~~~~~~~~~

GR

REALITY

~~~~~~~~~~~~~~~~~

The Seacastle Mysteries
Book 7

PJ Skinner

ISBN 978-1-913224-55-4

Copyright 2025 Parkin Press

Cover design by Mariah Sinclair

Discover other titles by PJ Skinner

The Seacastle Mysteries
Deadly Return (Seacastle Mysteries Book 1)
Eternal Forest (Seacastle Mysteries Book 2)
Fatal Tribute (Seacastle Mysteries Book 3)
Toxic Vows (Seacastle Mysteries Book 4)
Mortal Vintage (Seacastle Mysteries Book 5)
Last Orders (Seacastle Mysteries Book 6)
Lethal Secret (Seacastle Mysteries Book 8)

Purrfect Crime (A Christmas Mystery novella)

Mortal Mission A Mars Murder Mystery written as Pip Skinner

Green Family Saga (written as Kate Foley)
Rebel Green (Book 1)
Africa Green (Book 2)
Fighting Green (Book 3)

The Sam Harris Adventure Series (written as PJ Skinner)
Fool's Gold (Book 1)
Hitler's Finger (Book 2)
The Star of Simbako (Book 3)

The Pink Elephants (Book 4)
The Bonita Protocol (Book 5)
Digging Deeper (Book 6)
Concrete Jungle (Book 7)

Sam Harris Adventure Box Set Book 2-4
Sam Harris Adventure Box Set Book 5-7
Sam Harris Adventure Box Set Books 2-7

Also available as AI narrated audiobooks on YouTube and from my website

Go to the PJ Skinner website for more info and to purchase paperbacks directly from the author:
https://www.pjskinner.com

Dedicated to my wonderful father, who has encouraged and supported me all my life.

He also does the excellent final proofing on every book I write.

Kim

Best wishes

Chapter 1

Winter gripped Seacastle in its icy claws and tried to squeeze the life out of it. The bleak grey seas whipped the Victorian pier without mercy, driving people indoors to watch television and drink endless cups of tea. The loose sash windows in my small terraced house, affectionately known as the Grotty Hovel, rattled at night, making us hide under the covers. The house felt cavernous and empty despite the presence of my partner Harry Fletcher and of Hades, our rescue cat. The large hole had opened up in the absence of my stepson, Mouse, the son of my ex-husband, DI George Carter and his deceased first wife. Mouse had become part of my household, and the owner of a large piece of my heart, after breaking in to my house one night. Somehow, he never left. I had known I would miss him when he left for university, but I hadn't realised how much. I counted off the days until his next half-term, with the impatience of a child waiting for Christmas.

Mouse's absence exacerbated my usual winter blues. The short chilly days and the long dark nights brought back whispers of the clinical depression I had suffered in the past. The tendrils penetrated my soul and made me ungrateful for the things I had, and long for the things I had lost, or the status to which I aspired. Harry tolerated me and dragged me out of the house on the least pretext. His breezy good humour often blew away my misery for a few hours. I wondered how he could stand my black dog days, but he told me he loved all my parts, the bad, the good, the worn out, and those still in working order.

'Like my old van,' he said, half in jest.

I wasn't insulted. He loved that van with a passion before it broke down for good. Harry could be rather blunt, a legacy from his days in the armed forces, but he had learned to share his feelings with me. Nobody had my back like him. He acted like a Kevlar suit, shielding me from the slings and arrows of life. It was no surprise he encouraged me to apply as location manager to the Sloane Rangers reality show when the producers had decided to film a few episodes in Seacastle. I didn't need much prompting. The period following the Christmas rush in Seacastle always depressed me. My vintage furniture shop, Second Home, had no central heating and the sun only warmed it two hours a day, if it bothered to poke out from behind the clouds. We used an ancient fan heater in desperation on the coldest days, but the ill-fitting windows in the Vintage Café upstairs released any heat generated by it. I had planned to replace the windows with double glazed ones, but the quotes had almost given me a heart-attack. I had paid off my overdraft at the bank after a decent festive season, and I had no intention of getting into debt again if I could avoid it.

Sloane Rangers was a long running television show with a massive following. The cast consisted of young people who aspired to life in the fast lane. They had spent the last eight years exposing their dreams and fears to a nationwide audience, bickering their way into people's hearts. Love affairs had sprung up and burst apart in full view of the rabid fans. I wondered if they could be real, as the hysterical reactions were often ludicrous. Sloane Rangers made East Enders appear normal. The whole town was agog at the prospect of having the show's celebrities in their midst. Everywhere I went, including at my shop, the imminent arrival of the cast and crew dominated conversations.

Despite my reluctance to emerge from the cosy confines of the Grotty Hovel, I had to turn up there most days to run it. I set out along the promenade, leaving the car at home, which I often did to force myself to get some exercise. My long winter coat kept out most of the chill as I strode along, avoiding the dogs walking their owners. The seagulls wheeled overhead, emitting mournful cries at the lack of pickings, and patrolling for a kind soul with some crusts in a plastic bag. The clean smell of the sea lifted my spirits as I gazed out at the wind farm shrouded in low cloud.

As I reached the shop, I peered in through the window and spotted my friend Roz Murray, wife of Ed the fisherman, and the fountain of all local gossip, standing behind the counter chatting to Ghita Chowdhury. They were my best friends and worked shifts at the shop and café when I had to be elsewhere, such as on a clearance mission with Harry and the new van. Ghita was officially single, but she had a complicated arrangement with the gay couple who ran the high-end Surfusion restaurant almost opposite my shop. At one stage they had talked about having a baby together, but like many of Ghita's ideas, it turned into a pipedream. She also produced a constant stream of delicious and original cakes from her kitchen for the Vintage Café upstairs, so I couldn't fault her. We had great difficulty resisting her wares when we had a coffee break, which was often. The two women greeted me with shivers as I entered the shop.

'Blimey,' said Roz. 'It's freezing in here. Shall we risk an hour with the fan heater on?'

'I've worn my thermals,' said Ghita. 'And I'm still ice cold.'

'I thought you'd put on weight,' said Roz, smirking.

'At least I don't smell of fish,' said Ghita.

'Honestly, you two. Give it a rest. They'll be calling you in as extras on Sloane Rangers soon.'

'I don't know how they stand it,' said Ghita. 'All that bickering.'

'You don't imagine it's real, do you?' said Roz.

Ghita rolled her eyes.

'It's a reality show. Of course it's real.'

'Not really,' I said. 'I heard they generate drama by lying to the cast to create conflict.'

'But are they allowed to film fake scenes?' asked Ghita. 'It's supposed to be real life.'

'It's a TV show,' said Roz. 'Everyone knows the storylines are manufactured.'

'Not all of us do,' said Ghita. 'Anyway, we love the drama.'

'And by we, you mean Kieron Hissy-fit Murphy and Rohan Grumpy Patel?' said Roz, referring to the owners of Surfusion, a couple who thrived on conflict. 'Their life resembles a reality show.'

'You're as bad as they are,' I said. 'Maybe you and Ed should apply.'

Ghita snorted.

'Or star in a new program called Fisherman's Fiends.'

Roz laughed.

'Ed would love that. He'd get lots of new clients.'

'Will you apply for an interview?' said Ghita.

'I already got one,' I said. 'I guess my background at 'Uncovering the Truth' must have impressed them.'

'That's fantastic,' said Ghita. 'When is it?'

'Later this morning. I'll walk up to the Cavendish Hotel.'

'Do you plan to wear that?' said Roz, glancing at my outfit.

'What's wrong with it?' I said,

I had worn wool trousers with a cute Norwegian cardigan and a pair of pixie boots. I thought I rocked the outfit.

'Don't listen to her. You look fabulous,' said Ghita. 'Although putting your hair in a bun would give a more professional vibe.'

I found a scrunchy in my bag and pulled my hair into shape. Then I examined my reflection in the mirror behind the counter. With my hair up and a touch of lipstick, I felt instantly more ready. Roz pursed her lips, having lost interest in my appearance.

'You wouldn't think they'd be that keen on having a sleuth around,' she said. 'Imagine all the dirt they've had to sweep under the carpet. I bet there are many stories they wouldn't want leaking out to the press.'

'Maybe they think Tanya's a fake researcher too,' said Ghita.

I rolled my eyes at her.

'Since we're having a morning of fake sales, why don't we take the fan heater upstairs to the Vintage and have a cup of coffee? What's the cake of the week, Ghita?'

'Lemon and lime sponge with a touch of limoncello and some lime zest in the frosting.'

'When life gives you lemons,' I said.

Chapter 2

I quickened my pace as I strode along the promenade to the Cavendish Hotel. The westerly breeze at my back whipped my hair out of its bun into my face and I stopped to bind it into a pony tail. Purple clouds hung low over the wind farm south of Seacastle, but the skies over the town were blue and clear. I watched the seagulls bickering on the pebble bank before setting off again. Anticipation made my stomach churn as I neared the hotel. The Victorian hotel fronted onto the Steine gardens. It featured ivy draped balconies, and heavy wood and glass doors. I brushed beads of sweat off my forehead as I entered the lobby. Not late, but flustered, hoping for a representative of Sloane Rangers to make themselves known.

When no one appeared, I examined the decor. The interior of the Cavendish had a mixture of faux art nouveaux and art deco fittings which hadn't been updated since the eighties. A wooden fireplace on the far wall was framed by flowered tiles. Above the mantelpiece, a painting of a ship navigating stormy seas took pride of place. The upholstery on the chairs and sofas scattered around the ample lobby mirrored the diamond patterned carpet and a vintage magazine rack sat between them. An annex to the back contained help-yourself tea and coffee, under the gaze of a Churchill portrait in which he smoked a fat cigar. A red letterbox sat in the wall, a receptacle for the keys of people leaving the hotel.

A voice behind me made me jump.

'Tanya? It's Natasha Golova. I used to work with you on *Uncovering the Truth*. Well, not with you exactly. I worked on the production team.'

'Natasha? What a lovely surprise! Of course I remember. We had some epic evenings together, drinking champagne and watching Russian movies I couldn't understand. I didn't realise you were working on this show.'

'Yes, I'm the health and welfare director.'

Her tone struck me as odd. It contained an element of regret, or perhaps resentment? I couldn't tell. I could find out later. We hugged briefly and beamed at each other. I found her appearance slightly unnerving as she had acquired filler enhanced lips, and her doll-like face did not move when she smiled. Natasha did not notice my consternation and linked her arm through mine, leading me into the lift. The door closed, and we rose to the top floor together. The lift shuddered to a halt, and we stepped into a pink corridor.

'We've booked the entire floor for the Seacastle episodes,' said Natasha. 'It's easier to keep tabs on everyone that way.'

She sounded like a teacher on a school trip. I had tried not to have any preconceptions about the characters in the cast, but having watched the programme often, found it hard to remain neutral. The only person I liked was Daisy Kallis, and that preference had been influenced by Mouse and Harry, both of whom had crushes on her.

Natasha knocked on the door of the Grenville suite.

A loud, impatient voice boomed out from behind it. 'Come!'

Natasha rolled her eyes.

'He likes to intimidate people.'

I swallowed and plastered a smile on my face. I crossed the room to where an absurdly handsome, silver-haired man with crystal blue eyes sat at a table covered in electronics of various types. He didn't stand up, but the giveaway bulges in his shirt told me he worked out. His attention was fixed on a tangled heap of cords and chargers and he grunted with frustration as he failed to extract the one he wanted. His eyes flashed under his furrowed brow and knitted eyebrows. I offered him my hand, but he did not take it.

'Tanya Bowe,' I said.

'Can you untangle wires?' he asked in an American accent. 'So much for the paperless office. Even if I can start my laptop, I can't remember any of my passwords. My printed documents never got tangled up like this.'

I took the proffered bundle and, being fairly dextrous, I soon removed the cord he needed. He beamed.

'You're the local paparazzo? I don't think I've come across you before. Have you always been a journalist? I'm sure I'd remember such a beautiful one if we'd met before.'

I ignored the obvious line.

'My specialism is investigative work. You might have seen me in *Uncovering the Truth?*'

His eyebrows raised high on his craggy face.

'You worked on that show? Natasha, we are in the presence of royalty. Rustle up some coffee.'

A flash of annoyance crossed Natasha's face.

'We've met before. You forget I worked on that show too.'

'Not at all. You made me watch the reruns.'

She sniffed and turned to me.

'Do you still drink espresso?'

'I've up sized to lattes these days, thanks,' I said.

'A latte it is then.'

She slammed the door as she left. I had forgotten how touchy she could be. The man stood beside my chair.

'Alone at last,' he said. 'I'm Brad Fordham, by the way, out of Dallas, Texas.'

He twinkled his eyes at me. 'What do you know about our show?'

'I watch it with my stepson. He's a big fan,' I said, trying to edge further away from him.

'But you're not? I get that. Reality TV is not for everyone. I like to think we're a relatively high-class outfit.'

'Oh, I didn't mean—'

'That's all right. I know class when I see it. What do you need from us?'

'I heard you were searching for someone to act as a local liaison. I've lived here for most of my life and I can recommend locations for filming.'

'It's not that simple you know. You'll be in charge of logistics and crowd control when we film onsite. Local interest can be quite overwhelming sometimes.'

I tried to imagine seething hoards in Seacastle disrupting filming, but I failed. The last time they recorded a series here, the locals had been totally uninterested, and often ruined scenes by walking through them during filming. However, if Roz and Ghita's reactions were typical, interest levels might be increased for Sloane Rangers.

'I think I can manage that. I have scouted some great locations already. A pub, a restaurant and a couple of cafes.'

'Great. Seacastle is not iconic, but it's cheap to film here and there are fewer distractions for the cast members. You'll need to deal with the permitting first.'

'Permitting?'

'We need permits from the council for filming on the street. Do you have any contacts there?'

Ghita had worked for the council and knew everyone in the permitting department, so I nodded.

'I'm confident I can expedite the permits for you if you give me a list as soon as possible. If I get the job, I'd like to write a couple of articles for the local newspaper, if that's okay?'

His brow furrowed again.

'Nothing intrusive,' I added. 'Puff pieces.'

He stared intently at me while I spoke, and I could feel the colour rising in my cheeks. He smirked at my discomfort.

'I can't think of anyone better qualified. I'm interested to hear more about you. We'll email you a contract as soon as we can. You'll need to sign an NDA if that's okay?'

'No problem. Your secrets are safe with me.'

I placed the remaining unravelled cord on the table, rolled into a neat parcel.

'Perfect. See you soon, kitten.'

Kitten? Tiger would have been more appropriate, I felt. As I left, I met Natasha in the passageway. She handed me my latte.

'Coffee to go?' she said.

'It looks that way.'

'Did he make a pass at you?'

I shook my head, but I blushed.

'He normally prefers them skinny. You need to have red lines with Brad,' she said, noticing my pink cheeks. 'He won't take no for an answer.'

'Thanks for the tip. It's nice to be working with you again.'

She put her hand on my arm.

'He's not the only one. Don't let down your guard. They're not a nasty bunch, but there are powerful undercurrents. You don't want to find yourself out of your depth.'

Before I could answer, she had gone, wobbling on her high heels in the thick hall carpet.

Having successfully navigated my interview with Brad Fordham, I strolled back along the promenade to Second Home. It sat at the shabby end of Seacastle High Street, its neighbours mostly charity shops and a handy branch of the Co-op. January was never a wonderful month for sales of vintage bric-a-brac. Our clients disappeared into their houses after Christmas, padlocking their wallets against temptation. A chill had descended with north-east winds and showers of painful hail catching the unwary on the promenade, sending them scurrying into the Victorian wind shelter, which punctuated it. I stopped to gaze at the exquisite antiques in the window of the Asian Emporium, owned by our friends Grace and Max Wong. They had gone on holiday to Singapore to see relatives of theirs who had also abandoned Hong Kong. I wished we could afford to fly to a sunny beach for a month to avoid the worst of the winter.

If Brad gave me the job, I would at least have something to distract me from the winter weather. I racked my brain for any memories of Natasha from my time at *Uncovering the Truth*. Her new face had confused me, but I remembered her having a medical background. But what was she doing working as the director of health and welfare? Perhaps she had not fulfilled the requirements to practise medicine in the UK yet. I arrived at the shop and pushed my way through the door. Roz looked up from the magazine she was reading.

'How did it go?' she said, pushing back her mop of yellow curls. 'Did you get the gig?'

'Did you see Daisy Kallis?' said Ghita, emerging from the toilet. 'Was she at the hotel?'

She stood on her toes in excitement.

'Yes, they practically offered me the job, and no, I didn't spot Miss Kallis.'

'When will they inform you about the job?'

My phone pinged in my pocket. I took it out and tapped the screen.

'They already have. They've sent me a contract.'

'That's fantastic,' said Roz. 'You'll sign of course?'

'I'm not sure yet. I have to discuss it with Harry. Anyway, I don't have any experience in permitting.'

Ghita squeaked.

'I do. Oh, please let me help.'

She flashed her big brown eyes at me.

'I'll have to agree to the contract first.'

Chapter 3

Shortly after my interview with Brad Fordham, Harry announced he had accepted a contract to clear a house outside the hamlet of Hammerpot. I felt as if I had won the jackpot twice in a week. Clearances always lifted my mood and the chance of obtaining some fresh stock for Second Home filled me with excitement.

'Who owns the property?' I said.

'Some company in the Bahamas,' said Harry. 'If it's merely for investment purposes, it may be full of IKEA bookshelves and not much else.'

'You never know. Maybe someone left a Faberge egg on one of them.'

'Well, I accepted the job, so we'll soon find out.'

We set out two days later on a frosty morning painted the fields white. The wipers dislodged the ice from the van's windscreen, clearing the view from the cabin. The stark outline of the deciduous trees bordering the road contrasted with the flouncing fronds of the dark green pines. They blurred into one as we sped along the road to Littlehampton, sated with some delicious bacon butties, our fingers leaving fatty imprints on the steering wheel and dashboard. The lingering odour of bacon gave the cabin the air of a greasy spoon café and it made me nostalgic for Harry's original van, which he had inherited from an uncle in the East End. Its replacement had not been new either, and the fingerprints detracted little from its total lack of glamour. The best thing about it was a retro-fitted cassette deck which vindicated my decision to hang on to all of my old tapes, years after everyone else had thrown theirs out.

I guess I'm a bit of a Luddite, but I don't believe in throwing functional things away. My late-lamented parents brought me up with the make-do-and-mend culture of WWII, and I struggled with hoarder leanings. The Grotty Hovel strained at the seams with rescued items, including Hades, the cat. My original vinyls were among the treasures I rescued from the beige villa where George and I attempted to be married for a decade. Harry had now replaced George in my affections and to everyone's surprise, my sister Helen had stepped into the breach with George. It's not like I hadn't warned her all about him, but they were happy, so I didn't mind. I slipped in a cassette of Louis Armstrong and Ella Fitzgerald and turned up the volume.

We arrived at a cute hamlet with thatched houses and drove through to the other side where Harry turned up a short driveway to an enormous modern house with double glazing and a two-car garage. I tried not to sigh out loud as I took in the unlikely hunting ground. I wondered how the builders had got planning permission for the monstrosity in such a rural setting. Vintage furniture rarely hung out in modern houses with trophy garages, but I lived in hope. The manicured lawns were a sure sign of occupancy. Harry did a three-point-turn to position the van doors in front of the garage and jumped out onto the driveway. I descended with more caution and stood in front of the house, taking in its expensive finishings. As always, before my first glance inside a property, my heart rate had risen and my anticipation had sharpened. I rubbed my hands together and Harry snorted.

'Calm down,' he said. 'You're like a sheepdog who has spotted a flock of sheep. There may be nothing here for us.'

'My glass is always half full,' I said.

'That's why you spend your life in the toilet.'

I punched his shoulder, not hard enough to hurt his massive muscles, but he jumped away, rubbing it in fake pain. I rolled my eyes at the exaggeration and walked up to the door with its lion-head knocker and 'no junk mail' letter box. The brass doorbell resisted my finger. I put my ear to the door and pushed it again to check it worked and heard its chime echo in the hallway. The slippers which shuffled silently to the door did not warn me of its impending opening. I fell inside, grabbing a coat stand in the hall and bringing its contents down over me. I lay prostrate at the feet of a thin girl in a ratty dressing gown.

'I'm used to having men prostrate themselves at my feet,' she said. 'But this is a first.'

I tried not to laugh, but she started to giggle and set us all off. Harry, his face creased with mirth, reach down and offered me his hand. I staggered to my feet and was astonished to find the exquisite face of Daisy Kallis, the TikTok influencer and reality TV star in front of me. She bit her lip to stop herself giggling and offered me her hand.

'I'm Daisy.'

I took it and felt the slim, bony fingers warm in mine. I smiled.

'And I'm Tanya. This is Harry. We're here to do the clearance.'

Harry seemed unable to move. His mouth hung open in amazement like Hades waiting for a piece of chicken.

'You certainly cleared the coat stand,' she said. 'I'm impressed.'

She grinned. Her chocolate-coloured eyes sat in a heart-shaped face surrounded by soft, light brown curls. If I fancied women, I would have fallen for her right there and then. Harry seemed thunderstruck. We were besotted in an instant. No wonder she had a squillion followers.

'No encores,' I said. 'I could break a hip. Is it for removal? The coat stand?'

'Um, yes, everything is. My ex-left all his furniture behind when he dumped me. I'm selling the house too. I never liked it. Zak had it furnished by a designer. It cost him a fortune.'

I stifled a gasp. Daisy Kallis and Zak Kenton were the perennial lovebirds of the Sloane Rangers cast. The press would have a field day if they discovered the truth. It wouldn't be from me, though.

'And where will you go?' said Harry.

'Back to Greece. I'm from there you know.'

'I didn't, but I do now.'

'May we look around?' I asked.

'Sure. Make yourself at home. I'll get dressed.' She stopped halfway up the stairs and leaned over the bannisters. 'Would you like a cup of coffee?'

'That would be most welcome, thank you,' I said.

Why was I being so formal? A simple yes would have done. Harry made a face at me and I shrugged. Daisy wafted upstairs, and I folded the coats which I had knocked to the ground. I realised that both the coat stand and the hall dresser with a small central mirror were vintage Edwardian Bentwood pieces, and wondered what other treasures we might find. Grace Wong would surely take them off my hands as soon as she saw them in the window of my shop. While Daisy got dressed, we wandered around the ground floor, touching the treasures and making noises of approval. I gazed around the living room. Zak's designer had done his job with care. The house reeked of ostentatious good taste. Even Harry seemed impressed.

'I'm ignorant about antiques,' he said. 'But I know class when I see it.'

He raked me with a glance, as if I hadn't understood the reference.

'Honestly,' I said. 'Haven't I taught you anything? This place is like Grace's shop on acid. We can't afford any of this stuff. We need to come clean.'

'Zak must be made of money.'

'He gets over ten million dollars a movie.'

'No wonder he left everything behind. It's probably not worth fighting Daisy for it.'

The sound of spoons against glass alerted us to Daisy's presence in the kitchen. I left Harry to finish his survey of the contents and pushed my way through the swinging door. The smell of freshly brewed coffee hit me as I entered, making my head swim with its rich aroma. Daisy smiled at my expression of ecstasy.

'It's Jamaican Blue Mountain. Only the best for Zak.'

As she reached into the fridge, her wraparound skirt fell open and revealed skinny white legs covered in old yellow bruises. I swallowed a gasp and pretended to admire the Gaggia Brera on the counter, pristine and gleaming like the rest of the kitchen which resembled an advertisement in *Architects Digest*.

'Did he buy the coffee machine too?'

She laughed.

'No, that's mine. He only drinks bourbon.'

'I thought his body was a temple,' I said, quoting some ludicrous interview he had given on a red carpet.

'More like a shrine to alcohol. How do you like your coffee?'

'Milky please, no sugar.'

'And Harry?'

'Same with sugar, please.'

She put a jug of milk under the spout and frothed it before pouring it into our cups. I took them into the living room where Harry lounged in a reclining chair. He pressed the panel to bring it upright, looking as guilty as Hades after he had been accused of leaving a half-eaten mouse on the kitchen floor.

'Sorry,' he said. 'Making sure it was working.'

He had a sip of coffee. His eyebrows shot up.

'Blimey. That's delicious.'

'It is wonderful, isn't it?' said Daisy, hugging her cup. 'I shall miss it when I move.'

'Why don't you take a supply to Greece?' I said.

'It's part of my old life. I'm giving up my online career. I've made enough money to revive the family olive business, so I'm returning home to help my father get it going again.'

Her skirt had fallen open again, and I saw Harry glance at the bruises on her legs.

'What will Zak do when he finds out you've sold all his stuff?' he said.

'But I'm not selling it. I'm giving it to you,' she said.

'Won't he be annoyed? I've heard he can be a bit of a hothead,' I said.

'Oh, he'll probably kill me,' she said, laughing. 'But he'll need to find me first.'

'I'm not sure we can take anything under those circumstances,' said Harry, creasing his forehead.

'It's up to you. Otherwise, I'll give it to the new owners of the house.'

'What if we give a part of the proceeds to charity?' I said. 'There's a women's refuge in Seacastle.'

I couldn't help glancing at her legs and she caught my eyes flickering. Her cheeks became pinker, and she swallowed. I wondered if she would throw us out. She put on a fake smile instead.

'Is that where you live?' she said. 'I'm supposed to be doing an episode of Sloane Rangers there soon.'

'I know. I'll be working with you.'

'You will? I had no idea. That's fantastic. We can have lots of fun.' Then her face fell. 'As long as I can avoid Zak. I don't want to stay in the Cavendish Hotel with the others.'

I couldn't stop myself.

'You'd be welcome to stay with Gladys next door to us if you don't fancy a hotel,' I said. 'She has a couple of spare rooms and she needs a lodger. And I'll drive to the set every day if you need a lift.'

Her eyes opened wide.

'You will?'

'Yes, I'll be working as location manager and doing cast interviews for the local paper.'

She smiled.

'That sounds fantastic.'

'Here's my card.'

I reached over to hand it to her, and she stashed it in the pocket of her blouse. I imagined it would go straight in the bin when we left. Harry stood up.

'We'd better get started,' he said. 'Before you two move in together.'

'He's jealous,' I said. 'We'd love for you to come and visit anyway. My stepson, Mouse, would be ecstatic. I'd better help Harry before he gets grumpy.'

Harry drew his eyebrows together, pretending to be cross. Daisy let out a tiny gasp when she noticed his face. An expression of alarm crossed her face, and she pulled her legs under her on the seat, grabbing her knees.

'Take it all,' she said, gesturing at the furniture, her eyes strangely blank. 'Take the lot. I never want to see it again.'

Chapter 4

On our way home from the clearance, we were each preoccupied with our own thoughts. I couldn't get over the purple bruises which punctuated Daisy's slim legs. They were too random and numerous to be caused by a fall. I knew that habitual abusers never went for their victim's face if they could help it, thus avoiding detection. I couldn't understand why a rich, independent woman would let someone use her as a punchbag. It wasn't as if she couldn't afford to leave him. And she didn't have any children to tie her to their relationship. Harry sighed and ran his hand over his bald pate.

'He's lucky he wasn't at home. I'd have punched his lights out.'

'I'm not sure you would have helped much.'

'No, but I'd feel a lot better than I do now. Have you told Gladys?'

'Not yet. Do you think Daisy meant it, about staying next door?'

'I guess it will keep her safe from Zak in the evenings for the time being.'

'And later?'

'I don't know. I can monitor things at the set.'

'You're taking the job?'

'I think so. I'm not sure I need the drama. Now I know Daisy and Zak are separating. I think it's a recipe for conflict and I don't fancy being in the middle of it.'

He frowned.

'You could be right. Um, did you think she was rather thin? I mean compared to the last series.'

'Maybe. But they say television adds ten pounds. Perhaps that's why.'

'Hm. She has lost more than ten, if you ask me.'

I was still procrastinating when I received a call from Jim Swift the proprietor of the local newspaper, the Seacastle Echo. We had last collaborated on a series of articles covering the finals of the Tribute Show held at the Pavilion Theatre on the promenade. One contestant had been murdered, which had generated far more interest than the coverage of their careers. Jim had sold his version to the national press and generated income for the Echo. We had maintained contact since then, and he had helped me solve a murder (although not on purpose). When I saw his name on the screen, I felt suspicious of his motives. Everyone in town knew about the Sloane Rangers' arrival. Was he gunning for a scoop? My hand hovered over the phone, but I answered it anyway.

'Hi there. It's Jim Swift.'

'Jim. What can I do for you?'

'There are rumours you have a gig with the Sloane Rangers.'

Roz! I should have known. Her nickname was Foghorn for a reason.

'I might have had an offer. What can I do for you?'

'Let's have a cup of coffee? My treat.'

'How about the Ocean Café?'

'I'd rather have one at the Vintage.'

Jim had a reputation as a miser. I had no intention of providing free coffee for a meeting where he would benefit from my knowledge. His tone of voice had already alerted me to his keen interest.

'It's minus three degrees in the shop and the fan heater is a fire hazard.'

He sighed.

'Okay, the Ocean it is. Can we meet in half an hour?'

'I'll need an hour.'

'Okay, see you then.'

After finishing up my accounts, I made my way to the pier and strolled along the boards to the end where the Ocean Café teetered over the sea. It had a double layer of round windows like a cruise ship and an Art Deco shape. I headed for the mezzanine level where they served expensive coffee on velvet sofas shaped like seashells with a free view of the waves thrown in. I mounted the stairs with the elaborate fish wallpaper and spotted Jim waiting for me at one table. He jumped up when I arrived and came over to give me a peck on both cheeks. I winced at the smell of his breath and tried to smile.

'You're glowing,' he said. 'I hear you have a new man.'

'Does Roz tell you every detail of my life?' I asked.

He bit his lip to stifle a laugh.

'Almost. But you can fill me in on anything she's missed.'

I shook my head and manoeuvred my way onto the sofa, sitting as far from him as I could. A young waiter took our orders, and I waited for Jim to spill the beans. He couldn't resist for long.

'I've heard rumours,' he said, chewing his thumbnail.

'Really? What sort of rumours?'

'About Sloane Rangers. A little birdy told me that one of the stars is leaving the show.'

The birdy couldn't be Roz. She had no idea about Zak and Daisy's split.

'Did they now?' I said. 'Have they given you the name of the star?'

'They don't have a name. You're the one with the golden ticket. Have you picked up any gossip?'

'I haven't started work yet, Jim. Your spies are jumping the gun.'

He sniffed.

'I need a scoop. The paper is struggling. Can't you tell me anything?'

'Not really. It would be unethical, but I'm allowed to write some articles about the cast and the Seacastle episodes if that helps?'

'Can I have them first?'

'Naturally, if you pay me for them.'

His face fell, and I laughed.

'It's okay. You don't have to pay me, but I want a cut if you syndicate the articles.'

'It's a deal. I'm sure you'll pick up some juicy titbits while you're working for them. I hear they're all at each other's throats.'

'Did your source tell you that too? Who are they, by the way?'

He tapped the side of his nose with his finger.

'A journalist never reveals his sources.'

'Do they work for the show?'

'I'm not telling you. Keep a close eye on the cast. Maybe there'll be a fight. That would shake up the ratings.'

'You'll be the first to know.'

'You're taking the job, then?'

'I guess I am.'

He clapped his hands together in glee. Whether at me taking the job or the arrival of our delicious coffees, I couldn't tell. He took a sip of his and licked the foam from his lips.

'Now we've dealt with business. Tell me about your new man. What does George think about it?'

When Jim left, still muttering because I wouldn't give him a scoop, I approached the manager of the Ocean to ask her if they could host a day of filming in the mezzanine area.

'Sloane Rangers? We'd bite your hand off for the chance,' she said. 'How long would it take?'

'I'll bring the producer here to scout out the place. He'll know how many hours they need for filming. I can't guarantee he'll go for it, though.'

'Bring him. What's the worst that can happen? And thanks.'

'Oh, no problem. Give me your number and I'll text you if we are coming.'

Chapter 5

I walked home from our meeting as the sun went down, shining straight into my eyes. I've always loved the promenade and its eclectic selection of humanity from the dog walkers to the winos gossiping in the wind shelters. I'd even made friends with a seagull. Well, I thought I had. Mouse thought Herbert was the dictionary definition of a fair-weather friend who only turned up because he knew I'd feed him. Unfair, but mostly true. Our cat Hades belonged in the same bracket, but Mouse and Hades pined for each other while Mouse studied at university, so their friendship was based on more than cupboard love.

I pondered the rumour which had reached Jim Swift, about someone leaving the show. Sloane Rangers had run for almost ten years, with the original cast little changed. The viewing figures sagged sometimes, but the producers always generated enough scandal to reinvigorate them for another season. I decided to visit the guru on the subject, my sister Helen. Most of the time, she let George, (yes, my ex-husband) operate the remote, but she only missed an episode of Sloane Rangers in an emergency. He couldn't understand her devotion to the show and regularly complained to me about it. I sympathised, but as the younger sister, my opinion did not count for anything. Still, it seemed as if her encyclopaedic knowledge of the show would finally prove useful. I texted her to ask if I could drop in for a cup of tea.

Helen opened the door with a smile on her face and gave me a warm hug. One of the best things about her moving down to Seacastle, apart from her taking George off my hands, was the improvement in our relationship. She had always been hypercritical of me and my choices, taking full advantage of her role as the elder sibling, but she had mellowed since her divorce. Her relationship with my ex-husband surprised everyone and scandalised a few, but they were better suited than we had ever been. I had soon adapted, and to tell the truth, George and I got on like a house on fire now we didn't live together anymore. Helen's recent insider knowledge of George had made her more sympathetic to our divorce too, so it was a win-win for all of us.

She led me into the sitting room and poured me a cup of tea before covering the teapot with a tea cosy shaped like a crown. She handed it to me, balanced precariously on a saucer. I knew they had been made by my niece Olivia in pottery class, so I didn't comment. Helen looked me up and down before speaking, alerting me to an incoming criticism.

'How's it going, stranger? I haven't seen much of you since Christmas. Is the shop busy?'

She knew January brought my sales crashing down. It was a veiled rebuke about my not visiting her often enough. Helen wielded her power over me like the sword of Damocles. A warning that our friendship could evaporate as easily as it had renewed. Luckily, I had the correct answer ready, an answer to knock her socks off, and neutralise the threat. I swallowed.

'I've been offered a job with the Sloane Rangers' show for their sojourn in Seacastle.'

Helen's eyes widened. She let out a gasp of excitement and knocked her tea off its wobbly saucer onto the carpet. I leapt forward with my napkin and dabbed ineffectually at it. Normally, she would have rushed to clear it up. Instead, she let me pick up the cup and drop some napkins on the spill. She sat open-mouthed. Finally, she ventured; 'Oh my goodness! How wonderful! I can't believe it. You'll take it, of course?'

I had intended to tease her, but I couldn't be sure she wouldn't have palpitations if I pretended not to accept.

'Of course,' I said. 'I start next week, but I know next to nothing about the show.'

'And you want me to fill you in?'

High spots of colour appeared on her cheeks.

'Yes, please. Can you explain who the main characters are and their relationships with each other? I don't want to seem totally ignorant.'

'But you've watched it before, haven't you?'

'Only occasionally. Mouse and Harry love Daisy Kallis, so when they're at home, they always tune in when it's on.'

'So, you know about Zak and Daisy? That's a start.'

I nodded. I was dying to tell her what I knew, but Helen and Roz loved to gossip together in the shop. How long would the breakup remain secret if the foghorn sisters shared that gossip? Helen shut her eyes and I could imagine the cogs whirling as she arranged her thoughts. She had an almost didactic memory of the happenings in reality shows.

'Well, Daisy's best friend is Freya Watson. She's the slightly plump girl, but exquisitely pretty, and she runs an online jewellery business. She hasn't got a boyfriend on the show. Everybody uses her as a sounding board.'

'Maybe the producer uses her so the viewers can keep up with developments.'

Helen tutted.

'Who told you that? She's a sympathetic ear. Nobody tells her what to do.'

'Who else is important?'

'Hector and Aeneas Vardy are the troublemakers of the group. The twins attended Eton together and work together as brokers in the City of London. They think they are better than everyone else and often play tricks on people using their identical appearances.'

'Who do they hang out with?'

'The giggle sisters, Milly Ponsonby and Rose Hart. They are cousins, I think. They're fashion students and they run a blog together. Milly had a crush on Ollie Matthews, but that fizzled out.'

'Anyone else?'

'There are loads of other cast members, but they are secondary. I don't know who will film at Seacastle. They usually only bring the most important people for offsite episodes. Maybe Hugo Granda and Carrie Atherton.'

'What's the background to the Sloane Rangers' visit to Seacastle? I'd have thought the Caribbean was more their bag.'

'I don't know. Maybe they craved nostalgia. A visit to the Lido, an ice cream on the promenade, a cream tea at the Ocean Café?'

'I'd better get cracking, then. I'm in charge of finding locations for them to film in. Ghita can help me obtain permits from the council for filming in public places, but I need to speak to the proprietors to pick dates for a visit. The Lido is closed until spring, so filming there may be tricky.'

'Will they need extras? I've always dreamed of being on television.'

I couldn't believe my ears. My staid sister wanting to be on a reality TV show. You can never predict the thoughts circulating in someone's head.

'I expect so. Shall I put you down on a list?'

'Could you? That would be wonderful.'

I smiled and sipped my tea. What on earth would George say if Helen worked as an extra? He would be sure to blame me, as usual. There was no point antagonising him more than I usually did. Perhaps I would get her some series merchandise instead.

I went straight home and binged three episodes from the last series of Sloane Rangers on my laptop. I sometimes watched the show with Mouse and Harry, but I had missed the subtleties of the show's relationships. I took an immediate dislike to the disdainful and snobby Vardy brothers, and felt disloyal to Daisy when I found myself drawn to Zak. He seemed far more vulnerable than I had remembered. I found it hard to imagine him as an abusive boyfriend. The giggle sisters were as shallow as puddles and only talked about boys, clothes and makeup. They ignored Freya Watson, who clung on to the periphery of the show, like somebody forced off a full life-raft.

Afterwards, I wondered how any of it could be real. Did people really talk like that? It seemed so over the top. My cell phone pinged at me and I glanced down at the screen. Daisy had sent me a photograph. She stood arm in arm with Gladys from next door, Gladys in a tweed coat and a woolly hat, and Daisy in a pair of shorts with a fleece hoody. I texted back with love heart emojis and she rang me immediately, burbling her joy.

'Thank you so much for suggesting it. Gladys and I are getting on like a house on fire. It's perfect here. I feel so safe.'

'I'm so glad to hear that. Will I see you on set tomorrow?'

'Absolutely. It will be such fun, you'll see. We're all going to be BFFs.'

Chapter 6

My first day on set proved to be eye opening and a little shocking. I arrived at first light, which, being winter in England, happened at just before eight o'clock. The cast had assembled in the lobby of the Cavendish Hotel. I recognised the main characters who stood together gazing at message boards on wheels which had been lined up on one wall. I glanced at their contents and was surprised to see what amounted to a complete story board on them. So much for reality TV. Mutterings of discontent issued from the group and a few choice swear words in fruity Etonian tones. I hovered behind them, uncertain if I should disturb them. Then Daisy Kallis turned around and spotted me. Her face lit up.

'You came! Brilliant. We're going to have such fun. Let me introduce you.'

I tried to be nonchalant but respectful as I met everyone. The Vardys shook the tips of my fingers for a split second before dropping my hand as if it was covered in excrement. Freya Watson and the giggle sisters, Milly and Rose air kissed me and then ignored me. Zak was the only person who smiled as he shook my hand.

'I hear you met Daisy at our house,' he said. 'She's doing it up or something. She says it's a secret.'

I almost choked on my reply, but I could see Daisy's look of entreaty out of the corner of my eye.

'I'm sure you'll find out eventually,' I blurted out.

Brad Fordham appeared and signalled for me to join him while the technicians moved the storyboards to the next room, out of the shot. Brad wore a cowboy hat and a shirt with tassels. Bizarrely, he reminded me of Dolly Parton. I walked as fast as I could without trotting.

'Miz Bowe. Glad you could make it. Find yourself a corner and watch the magic happen.'

I checked for a chair or a stool, but they were all occupied on set, so I upturned a flight case and perched on it, hoping I hadn't broken some cardinal rule. A shout of 'Silence!' cut off the burble of voices. Followed by 'Rolling'. The arc lights had been switched on and the formerly cool room became uncomfortably hot. No wonder people were dressed as if they were taking a Nile cruise. I wiped my brow with a tissue and tried not to fall off the flight case. The cast followed the story line etched out on the boards. Several cameos were filmed of hushed conversations behind other cast members' backs.

It all seemed pretty innocuous, and I had trouble staying awake. Soon I felt an urgent need to pee, but I couldn't cross the set. I hung on, getting more and more desperate. Just when I thought I might have an accident, Brad yelled, 'cut' and everyone relaxed. I dashed across to the reception desk where a harassed blonde receptionist tried to direct guests out of the side door to keep them from invading the lobby. A badge on her chest read Cheryl Barker. I shook my hand in the air and screwed my face up, which she correctly interpreted as a request for directions to the toilets. She pointed down a long corridor leading to the back of the hotel and grinned at me as I shuffled away with my legs semi crossed. Luckily, the ladies' toilet was empty. I took a volcanic leak and then mulled over what I had seen. I couldn't relate the bland scene to the episodes I had watched the night before. They were as drama packed as East Enders.

After washing my hands, I returned to the lobby where all hell had broken loose. Freya and Daisy were having a massive shouting match in one corner. The cameras were running, and Brad showed no sign of intervening. His face wore a smug expression.

'Isn't anyone going to stop them?' I said, blurting it out loud by mistake.

'Oh, I doubt it. Fights are box office,' said a voice.

The young receptionist, Cheryl, had positioned her chair so she could enjoy all the shenanigans in the lobby. She had a splendid view from behind her desk and she took full advantage of it.

'Do they fight often?'

'It's probably scripted,' she said, dropping her chin in her hands to watch the scene.

Zak grabbed Daisy from behind, putting his arms around her and lifting her away from Freya. Daisy screamed and wriggled, but she could not escape. Freya ran down the corridor toward the toilets. I waited for someone to follow her, but nobody moved. The giggle sisters approached Daisy, smoothing her hair and wiping away the tears from her cheeks while the cameras panned onto their faces.

'What was that about?' I asked Ollie Matthews who was lurking behind a large potted plant.

'I saw Brad whispering to Daisy. I think he dropped a cat among the pigeons,' he said. 'It's about time. This show is getting boring. We don't want to lose our viewers now do we?'

His tone dripped with sarcasm. He reminded me of my friend Kieron from Surfusion when he had a strop on.

'Which feline did he release?'

'You need to ask Freya that,' he said. 'It's more than my hide's worth to go around spreading gossip about the queen bees.'

'Is Freya a queen bee?'

'From what I hear, she's trying to take over the hive.'

He stalked off, one wrist in the air. I considered introducing Freya to Ghita. They both fancied men above their pay grade. Instead, I headed back down the corridor and found Freya weeping in the ladies' room. Her face had become red and puffy with emotion. She threw back her black curls and blew her nose into a crumpled ball of toilet paper.

'Are you okay?' I said. 'Can I help?'

'Who are you?' she said, sniffing. 'Did Brad send you?'

I couldn't tell if she had forgotten about meeting me already, or was pretending. I ploughed on.

'I'm Tanya, the Seacastle location manager. I saw your argument with Daisy and I thought you might need to talk about it.'

'What's there to talk about? Daisy Kallis is a cow, but everybody worships her. Somebody told her there was something going on between me and Zak, and she's pretending she cares.'

'You and Zak?'

'I don't know who told her. It's not true. Probably Brad. He loves to create conflict among the cast to get more drama in the episodes. It's the bread and butter of this series. I'll get blamed as usual. I'm the whipping horse of the cast.'

'What do you mean?'

'The audience needs someone to hate. I'm the sacrificial lamb since Fiona left. Before she went, all the storylines ended up with her to blame. She got sick of it. Now it's me. Brad wants me out because I'm too fat.'

'Too fat? You've got a superb figure.'

'He likes us to be more Kate Moss than Kate Winslett. The entire cast is injecting Ozempic.'

I tried not to appear startled.

'The entire cast?'

'Only the girls. And Ollie, because he doesn't enjoy being excluded.'

I searched her features for a sign she might be joking, but found none. She rinsed her face with cold water.

'Damn. I look like a pizza. Thank heavens for makeup. Let's get back. I don't want to give her the satisfaction of thinking I'm upset.'

'Are you sure you're okay?'

She gave me a stare.

'How good are you at keeping secrets?'

'I'm as silent as a tomb. I forget secrets as soon as I'm told them, which helps. I promise not to tell anyone. Cross my heart.'

She grinned.

'I'm developing a secret project which will blow the show apart. I'll tell you later if you like. I've got to go now. Brad will kill me if I don't get on scene in time.'

Intrigued, I followed her down the corridor to the lobby where everyone was settling back into their places to continue with the scene. Daisy and Zak were sitting at opposite ends of the lobby. Freya received a quick layer of powder to lower the colour of her face and sat halfway in between them, playing with Milly's hair. I returned to my flight case, which shifted under my weight, and I dropped my handbag as Brad yelled 'Shoot'. As I reached down to grab it, I cut my finger on something sharp.

'Ow!'

Brad turned around ready to complain, but the blood gushing down my finger startled him.

'That must be painful. Can you find Natasha upstairs in the clinic? She'll fix you up.'

The clinic? I wrapped a tissue around my finger and headed for the lifts. The tissue soaked through with blood and I put another on top. I felt queasy at the amount of blood. I arrived at the top floor and searched for the clinic. Somebody had stuck a piece of paper to a door using a lump of blue tack. The temporary sign read Sick Bay. I knocked on the door and opened it as Natasha trotted up to me.

'Hi Tanya. Apologies for keeping you waiting. I was in the toilet. What are you doing here?'

I stuck out my bloodied finger in its soggy tissues. She shook her head and made me sit down on the examination table.

'Did you try to cut off your own finger, or did you have help?' she said.

'I'm not sure. I snagged it on something when I tried to pick up my handbag.'

'Dangerous places film sets,' she said. 'If it doesn't stop bleeding, I may have to put a stitch in it.'

'I didn't know you had taken up medicine again,' I said.

She shrugged.

'I'm not licensed to practise in England, but Brad doesn't care. He says my training in Moscow was far superior to anything they get here. Don't worry. I send any serious cases straight to A&E.'

I surveyed the small room. It contained a cabinet full of pill bottles and medical paraphernalia on one side and a fridge on the back wall.

'Vodka?' I asked, pointing at it.

She laughed.

'Unfortunately, no. People's prescriptions mostly.'

'Is that where you keep the Ozempic?' I asked.

The blood drained from her face.

'Who told you that?'

'I guessed. The girls are thinner than they appeared last season.'

She avoided my eyes.

'It's Brad. He's determined to keep them all slim so they look good on screen.'

'Can I see it?'

She opened the door, and I saw a row of boxes lined up on one shelf.

'How do you know whose is whose?'

'The pens and the boxes all have stickers. There's no way of confusing them.'

'What's in the bottles?'

'Antibiotics.'

'That's quite a responsibility. I hope you're careful.'

'I really need this job. I've almost saved enough money to recertify myself here and then I'll return to medicine. There's no future for me in this industry. I shouldn't have stayed so long. Please don't tell on me.'

I sighed.

'Okay, but promise me you'll call an ambulance if anything happens to a member of the cast.'

'I'm an experienced nurse. I know the risks better than most. You have my word.'

Chapter 7

The filming continued. The scenes appeared pretty vanilla considering the tensions off camera. I wondered if Brad would engineer another spat between Daisy and Freya, but they avoided each other as much as possible. Freya seemed unaffected by her quarrel with Daisy and even exchanged a couple of covert glances with Brad. Knowing what I did about him, I wondered if I should intervene, but I had been confused by his mild manner and relaxed attitude around Daisy. She had told me he was dangerous, but none of this made sense.

I couldn't separate the acting from the real-life drama on set. I'm not sure what I had expected, but I hadn't realised the extent to which Brad and his editors pre-planned the storylines. The impression I had received from the TV show was a mirage, carefully choreographed by the producer and the editors to run seamlessly. The atmosphere made me feel nauseous, and I almost fainted with relief when Brad called a halt for the day.

He crooked his finger at me and examined my bandage.

'You'll live,' he said. 'Can you suggest somewhere to film a lunch, a pub night and a café scene asap?'

'I already have three places in mind. Would you like to see them?'

'Can we do one now? I'll bring one of the camera operators so he can take some still shots to use for the story boards.'

'Sure. The café stands at the end of the pier. It has the most fabulous views. It's like being on a cruise ship.'

'That sounds wonderful. Why don't you go ahead and we'll follow you there in the van?'

'Okay, but you can't drive down the pier. You'll have to walk.'

'We'll manage.'

I texted the manager of the Ocean and she replied with an unbroken line of open-mouthed emojis and OMGs. I asked her to keep the mezzanine clear so Brad could see it without clientele. Then I set out along the promenade. The sun was sinking rapidly, and the pier was bathed in golden light. I crossed my fingers Brad would come quickly and see how wonderful it looked. He caught up with me about halfway down the pier, his camera man trotting behind him, panting with effort.

'Wow! This is fantastic. I can't wait to see the café.'

'I think you'll like it. It has Titanic vibes.'

'Well, that's fitting, seeing as we are holed beneath the waterline and in danger of sinking.'

I must have seemed startled. He laughed and slid his arm through mine.

'Don't panic. That's why they brought me in. I'm definitely not going down with the ship.'

I felt a little uncomfortable with his proximity to me, but I couldn't think of a polite way to remove my arm from his grasp. His expensive cologne made my nose wrinkle as we walked along. He must have dropped the bottle on his suit from the strength of it. We did not enter the restaurant straight away but circled around it so the camera operator could record the views. The tide had come in and several fishermen dangled their lines in the water. The seagulls squawked at us, demanding a tax for our visit. Brad gazed down at the sea.

'It's so clear. I can see the bottom. It reminds me of a town I know back home.' He turned to examine the café. 'This place is perfect, by the way. Let's go in.'

The manager saw us enter and came over to shake Brad's hand. She led us up to the mezzanine where I had so recently been with Jim Swift and showed us around. Brad made the camera operator take shots from all angles.

'This is picture perfect,' he said. 'I hope your other choices are as good. What are you proposing?'

'Well, my friends Rohan and Kieron run a high-end seafood restaurant called Surfusion. The décor is extraordinary. It has Victorian taxidermy fish encased in the walls, so it feels as if you are eating under water. The food is fabulous too. I thought you could film a dinner there. They also serve lunch.'

'Can Surfusion be shut off for us?'

'I can ask them. They shut on Mondays and Tuesdays, so you could film then without disturbing anyone. Ghita can cook for the crew if you like.'

'Who's this Ghita person?'

'She's a friend of the owners and invents dishes with Rohan. She also bakes wonderful cakes which I sell in my café.'

He raised an eyebrow.

'You have a café? Why didn't you suggest it instead of the Ocean?'

'You told me you wanted spectacular locations. My café is above my vintage furniture shop in the High Street. It's cosy and has vintage furnishings, but it's not as glamorous as the Ocean.'

'Can we see it anyway?'

'Of course. It's nearby, and it's across the street from Surfusion if you want to see it too.'

'Can we do that tomorrow morning? It's time for a drink and I'd like to visit the pub you are recommending.'

'We'll need a lift out there. It's on the cliff edge.'

'It sounds amazing. I'll get the camera operator to drive. He can be the designated driver.'

'I can't stay late. My boyfriend is expecting me.'

'Can't you text him?'

'I'll do that when I need picking up. I'm sure he'd like to meet you.'

Brad gave me a sour smile.

'Let's go then,' he said.

We drove up to the Shanty's car park and started down the narrow path to the picturesque pub. It had tiny doors and windows because of the window tax, which was current when it was built, but that didn't detract from its appeal.

'This path is a death trap,' said Brad. 'What if a celebrity on my payroll takes a tumble?'

'What if they were pushed?'

'Don't even say that.'

We stooped under the lintel and entered the old-fashioned interior. Brad purred with pleasure as he inspected it. Ryan Wells, the owner of the Shanty, hovered at bar level in his specially adapted wheelchair. He shook hands with Brad and offered us a hot toddy.

'What's that?' said Brad.

'Whiskey, honey, lemon and hot water. It's a great winter warmer.'

'I'd prefer an Irish coffee if you can make one.'

'Sure. Shall I make you one too, Tanya?'

'Yes, please. Is Joy here?'

'She's visiting Budapest again.'

'Will she be back soon?'

'Let's hope so,' he said, winking at me.

I got the joke. Ryan and Joy were retired (supposedly) MI5 agents who had taken over the Shanty after Ryan had been paralysed in a shooting. Ryan had become worried about the safety of some of their missions and had taken me into his confidence 'in case we disappear and don't come back'. I felt proud they trusted me with this sensitive information and I never felt tempted to share it with anyone.

Brad directed the camera operator to take stills of the snugs and the window seats. Then we took our Irish coffees to a snug and sat alone. The camera operator had ordered himself a steak and kidney pie. The gorgeous smell of the pastry cooking in the kitchen almost made me faint. Brad showed no sign of hunger. I wondered if he also used Ozempic. I sipped my delicious coffee.

'Cheers,' said Brad. 'How was your first day? Sorry about the cat fight. I didn't realise Daisy and Zak were still an item. I might have dropped the ball on that one.'

'I heard you did it on purpose.'

He glanced at me from under his eyebrows, his ice-blue eyes twinkling with malice.

'Who told you that?'

'I don't remember, but I worked TV too. I know the rules of reality shows.'

A lie, but I hoped he might expand if he thought I might be complicit.

'Do you now? They brought me in to flog the dead horse. We do things differently in Texas. Everything's bigger, including the arguments. I know which buttons to press to force a reaction. And then we push through to the desired result to follow our predetermined story line. It's the Franken-scenes that make the episodes. Where we cut-and-paste boring lines for maximum awkwardness, humiliation and scandal long after the scene has been shot.'

'You mean the footage is real, but the product is not?'

'Something like that. Don't let it bother you. Set up the locations for the shoots and I'll do the producing.'

'What did you say to Daisy today?'

He laughed.

'I asked her about Zak and Freya playing house. I thought she knew, but I guess she didn't. Do you want another drink?'

'No thanks. I'll text Harry to come and get me and walk out to the car park to meet him.'

'So soon? Can't you stay for a while?'

'I'm sorry. We have something organised for this evening. Can we give you a lift somewhere?'

He pouted, and I almost rolled my eyes.

'No thanks. I'll get Finn to take me when he finishes his meal. The pub is fantastic, by the way. I'll book a day for filming with Ryan. Oh, and why don't you wait for me in the shop tomorrow? I'll film some brief scenes in the morning and then I'll come and see your café. What's it called?'

'The Vintage. It's above the Second Home furniture shop on the High Street.'

'Good name. Maybe we can eat at Surfusion?'

'I'll be there.'

I walked along the cliff path, mulling over my first day on the job. So much for the glamour of television. At least I would be well paid. I decided to keep my nose out of everyone's business, as hard as I might find it. Harry flashed the headlights of the Mini at me as I approached and as I stepped into the car, the gorgeous smell of fish and chips surrounded me.

'I knew there was a reason I loved you.'

'Cupboard love,' said Harry.

'The best sort.'

Chapter 8

The next morning, I arrived late to the shop after I had to clean up a macerated rodent which Hades had dropped on the kitchen floor. He liked to crunch up the head with his teeth and then eviscerate the bodies, leaving their tiny organs spread around like a gory version of 'Operation'. While I cleaned up, he wound himself around my legs, purring loudly. He even deigned to let me stroke him a couple of times before stalking away. I decided not to feed him if he had recently dined on mice. Fresh meat was far better for him than the packet stuff. I left Harry a note telling him to give Hades a sachet of rabbit when he got up. Harry had been using our van for deliveries between clearances, but he loved to sleep in when he didn't have to go anywhere.

I walked to work along the promenade, wrapped in my warmest down coat and wearing my favourite hat and scarf combo, presents from Harry. My face almost froze in the keen north wind and I had to wear my sunglasses to keep out the horizontal early sunshine. The tide had recently gone out, leaving rocks draped in kelp fronds with red anemones which resembled strawberry jellies stuck to their sides. Several rescue greyhounds sprinted in large circuits on the sand bar, encouraged by the shrill cries of their owners. I loved the dogs' enjoyment and the way they spent the rest of the day lying on their owners' beds comatose with laziness. I always fancied a greyhound, but Hades would have inflicted fatal wounds on any dog foolish enough to enter the Grotty Hovel.

I turned up King Street and headed for Second Home. Ghita had already arrived there and stood behind the counter, shivering. She had so many layers on she couldn't put her arms by her sides.

'Put the fan heater on,' I said. 'Brad Fordham is coming to inspect the shop and the Vintage. I didn't tell him we had no central heating.'

'Brad's coming here? How exciting! Do you think he'll try my cake?'

'He might do. Will you please let Rohan and Kieron know we will visit Surfusion at lunchtime? He wants to scout out the location for filming next Monday.'

'But it's not open on Monday.'

'I know. I thought you might cook for the cast if you're free?'

'Me? Of course, but Kieron may not let me. He will probably do it himself. He's quite keen on being famous. He fancies himself as a TV chef.'

'Why don't you pop over and tell them about Brad's visit? They can decide how they'd like to play it.'

Ghita squeaked with excitement and ran outside into the cold without her coat. At least Surfusion had central heating. I watched her jumping with excitement as she told our friends about the visit. Rohan leaned outside and gave me a thumbs up, his waxed moustache perched on his top lip. I left them to it and took out the furniture polish and a cloth. Then I methodically wiped down every single table and cupboard top with beeswax until the entire shop was filled with shiny wood. I used the extendable duster to clean the fisherman's floats and lamps, which dangled from the ceiling. Then I shook the rugs in the street and swept the wooden floor of the shop. It had recently been re-waxed, so it gleamed in the low sun light which entered.

When I finished the ground floor, I mounted the stairs to the café and performed the same routine. I also selected some of the best cups and saucers from our eclectic collection to use for coffee. Ghita's lime and lemon cake sat in the cabinet under glass with a plate full of her crispy almond biscuits. I resisted the temptation to try one. Staying slim in my shop required serious willpower. Then I switched on the fan heater to warm the shop. It spat out a sound like metal scraping, and smelled like burning rubber, but seemed to work okay. I made a note to buy a new one from Argos. Another expense. At least our newish van had not broken down. The old one had been a constant drain on our finances.

Ghita had not reappeared since she had gone over to Surfusion, but the complete absence of customers meant it didn't matter. She loved to hang out with Rohan and Kieron, plotting new menus and trying weird fusions of flavours in their kitchen. She had an extraordinary palate, matched by Kieron, so they were highly competitive. Rohan acted as peacemaker. I often thought he would have been the ideal partner for Ghita if he hadn't preferred men. She loved them both and spent a lot of time stroking Kieron's enormous ego so she could have time on her own with Rohan. I wished Prince Charming would ride into town and sweep her off her feet, but she liked her odd menage-a-trois and had stopped searching for him.

The doorbell clanged downstairs and Brad walked in followed by the camera operator.

'Wow! This is amazing,' he said, as I descended the stairs. 'It's like a yard sale indoors. But why is it freezing? And what's that burning smell? Are you setting fire to the furniture to stay warm?'

I sniffed the air and caught the acrid smell of melting plastic. I turned and dashed back upstairs followed by Brad. Smoke and flames billowed from the heater and the plastic covering had melted. Brad kicked the plug from the socket in one fluid movement. He spotted the fire extinguisher, which he grabbed and sprayed on the heater. One squirt put out the fire. He laughed and slapped his thigh.

'Why didn't we film this? The camera is never aimed at the correct angle in real life.'

'I'm so sorry,' I said. 'That vintage fan heater didn't last like the furniture. I tried to heat the café for you.'

'You certainly managed that,' he said, chuckling. 'Don't apologise. I haven't had such fun for ages. Maybe I should try to shoehorn a fire scene into the episode. Make someone a hero.'

'Well, this is the Vintage Café and downstairs is Second Home. The furniture in the café is for sale too, so people can buy their chair if it takes their fancy.'

'What a great idea! Let me think about using the shop and café together. Perhaps the Vardy twins and the giggle sisters can shop and gossip in here.'

He scratched his head.

'But the Vardys won't like it. They complain if the temperature is under twenty-four degrees centigrade.'

'I can't afford to put in central heating for filming.'

'Oh, I wasn't suggesting that. We've got some oil-filled heaters with us. I'll lend you a couple to use in the shop.'

'Are they expensive to run? Only—'

'Don't worry, they're pretty efficient. You'll appreciate the difference. Anyway, I'm sure our budget can stretch to paying for a warm set.'

'That would be wonderful. Poor old Ghita and Roz are freezing their socks off in here.'

'Is that one of Ghita's cakes in the cabinet?'

'Yes. Would you like a slice?'

'Not right now, but I'd love a taste.'

I cut him a sliver of the lemon and lime cake and gave it to him on a saucer. He picked it up and popped it into his mouth. His eyes grew round with wonder as the icing melted into his mouth.

'This cake is like nectar on my tongue. Where can I find Ghita?'

'She's across the road with the owners of Surfusion if you'd like to meet her.'

'What about the fan heater? Do you want to clear it away?'

'I'm starving. I'll deal with it later. Let's go.'

He grinned at me.

'I thought you told me it was a fusion restaurant. Aren't the portions tiny?'

'Yes, but I empty the bread basket of mini focaccias and seeded buns to fill myself up.'

'Not if I eat them first.'

Chapter 9

I had not eaten at Surfusion since we had staged a death for the Tarton Manor House Murder Mystery Weekend. Harry and I simply couldn't afford to eat there, except on special occasions. Also, Harry preferred restaurants with larger portions, so we ate elsewhere when we could afford it. I could still taste some of their dishes in my imagination, enough to make me drool spontaneously like Pavlov's dog. I had no idea if Brad would enjoy the food, but he seemed quite sophisticated, so I presumed he would appreciate the skill that went into preparing the dishes. I let him enter the restaurant first and heard him gasp as he gazed at the décor, thunderstruck. Most people reacted similarly when they first entered. It felt like entering an underwater grotto with large fish looming in the seaweed. The lacquered tabletops also had a marine theme. The interior had an immediate calming effect like diving in a submersible. The sound of waves breaking added to the feeling of relaxation. Finn, the camera operator, filmed the room with care from various angles while Brad stood at its centre like a small child marvelling at it. I liked him more immediately.

Kieron and Rohan waited at the counter, letting him take it all in. Surfusion had a similar effect on most clients and they had learned to give people space and time before offering them menus. Rohan caught my eye and gave me a thumbs up. I could see Ghita peeping around the door, her cheeks pink with excitement. Brad turned to me, his eyes shining.

'Words don't do justice,' he said. 'Why don't we order and I'll organise my thoughts?'

He whispered something to the camera operator, Finn, who nodded and left the restaurant. I felt sorry for Finn, whose name I had discovered only recently, missing the delights of Surfusion. Mind you, I had rather cockily assumed Brad would pay for our lunch, as my wallet echoed when I opened it. I coughed to attract his attention.

'I can't afford to eat here,' I said.

'Oh, this is my treat. I'm so excited you brought me here. That's payment enough.'

Rohan came forward and shook Brad's hand.

'We're so pleased to meet you,' he said, presenting Kieron and Ghita. 'It's such an honour.'

'Are you Ghita?' said Brad, looming over her. 'Your lemon cake took me on a trip to Paradise.'

Ghita blushed prettily.

'Thank you. It's the limoncello that makes it special.'

Rohan put us at a table beside the sea wall full of Victorian taxidermy fish. Brad took out his phone and snapped some pictures. Then he picked up the menu.

'Oh my. How will I choose?'

'Perhaps you would like to share several starters instead of a main course? Then you will understand what we offer, in case you want to eat here sometime,' said Rohan.

'Great. Is that okay with you, Tanya?'

'Perfect,' I said. 'You choose and I'll eat.'

He laughed.

'I love a woman who eats. They are so rare these days.'

I thought Ozempic might have caused that phenomenon, but I didn't comment. Brad called Ghita over and questioned her about the food. Kieron had retreated to the kitchen, or he would have resented her taking the spotlight. Rohan served the other customers who had no idea they had a celebrity in their midst. Meanwhile, I munched on the mini breads with dollops of butter and sniffed the air for evidence of our meal being prepared. I felt faint from hunger when the kitchen door opened and Kieron emerged with a tray of starters.

'I don't think I've ever seen such beautiful food,' said Brad, as Kieron positioned the plates on our table. 'I hope it tastes as good as it looks.'

'It does,' I said. 'They are wizards.'

'I'm going in,' said Brad, grasping his chopsticks and picking up a fat, battered prawn.

He bit into it and shut his eyes in bliss.

'Oh, good Lord,' he said. 'I think I died and went to heaven.'

I took one of the same prawns and had a similar reaction. The batter had a lemony taste as if it contained Fanta.

'These are spectacular.'

We worked our way through the plates, oohing and aahing and making chef's kiss gestures. I could see Kieron and Rohan elbowing each other and beaming in pleasure. Ghita hovered near the table, ready for any requests. Brad's mobile phone rang as I licked my fingers from mopping up the parsley sauce on a miniature filet of cod. He rolled his eyes, but answered it anyway.

'Can't it wait, Natasha? I'm—'

He dropped his chopsticks, which bounced off his plate and fell onto the floor. He swung sideways on his chair without picking them up, and stood holding his phone to his ear, his face pale.

'When? Where? Has she been taken to the hospital? We'll be right there.'

He bit his lip and searched for his wallet in his jacket.

'What's happened?' I asked.

'Freya Watson's collapsed. It sounds serious. They've taken her to Seacastle General.'

'That's terrible. Can I help?'

'You'd better come with me. I don't know the protocols for these matters.'

He beckoned Rohan over and gave him a credit card.

'I apologise, but we have to leave right away. Can you please charge my card?'

'Of course. Is everything okay?'

'Huh? Oh, it was. The food is out of this world. I can't believe we have to go now.'

'That's all right. You are welcome any time.'

'Thanks. We'll definitely film here, but can I talk to you about it another time?'

'Of course. Here's your receipt.'

Brad headed for the door. I shrugged at Rohan and followed him out.

'Can we take your car?' said Brad.

'I walked in today, I'm afraid. But I can call us a cab.'

'I'll give you a lift,' said Ghita.

We trotted to her car and got in. She reminded Brad to put on his seatbelt in her best schoolmarmish voice. Luckily, the lunchtime traffic had died down, and it took us less than ten minutes to arrive. We jumped out at the Accident and Emergency Department and, giving Ghita a wave, went inside to the reception desk. I smiled at the woman behind the counter.

'Hello, we're with Freya Watson. They brought her in from the Cavendish Hotel.'

The receptionist raised an eyebrow.

'And you are?'

'Oh, I'm Tanya Carter. And this is Brad Fordham. He's the producer of Sloane Rangers. Miz Watson is one of the main characters in the show.'

'That Tanya Carter?' she asked. 'We watched every episode, you know. You were brilliant.'

'It's so nice of you to remember.'

'You're welcome. Miss Watson is undergoing tests. You'll have to wait out here. I can let you through once they have stabilised her.'

'Will she recover?' said Brad.

'I don't know. Please sit down. Oh, and Mrs Carter?'

'Yes?'

'Can I have your autograph, please?'

'Really?' said Brad, miffed at the attention I was getting. But I gave her one with good grace and listened patiently while she told me how much her mother loved me. 'Uncovering the Truth' had struck a chord with people and their continued enthusiasm for the programme and all it stood for never failed to amaze me. It certainly proved useful over the years since I had finished on the show. I went to sit on an uncomfortable metal seat beside Brad, who shook his head at me, suppressing a grin.

'I didn't realise you were the famous one.'

'Neither did I. Did Natasha tell you what happened?'

'Only that they found Freya lying on her bed unconscious and bathed in sweat. I guess we'll soon find out.'

'I'm sure she'll be okay.'

But I lied. I wondered if Freya done something stupid, but it made little sense. The electric clock ticked loudly as we waited, each immersed in our own thoughts.

Chapter 10

Time stood still as we waited for news. I picked at my cuticles while Brad scrolled through his messages and watched memes of celebrities talking about themselves on chat shows. He kept standing and then sitting down again. Finally, a young woman in a white coat entered the reception area and approached the desk. The receptionist pointed at us, and Brad jumped up to greet her.

'Are you the doctor caring for Freya Watson?' he said.

'Yes, I'm Doctor Kumar. I understand you are the producer of the television programme.'

'That's me. I'm Brad Fordham.'

'Well, Mr Fordham. I'm afraid the news isn't good. She has slipped into a coma and she may not wake up.'

'A coma? I don't understand.'

'She came in with severe bradycardia. I was told that a member of the cast found Freya lying on her bed in her room, sweating profusely. She had passed out. We're doing all we can, but she may not recover.'

'But how, why?'

'I'm not sure. It may have been a cry for help. Did she have any mental health issues?'

'No. I don't think so. I—'

He froze.

'Can we see her?' I asked.

'Not yet. Once we've attached her to a drip and stabilised her, you may come in for a minute. Has she got any family? They should be alerted immediately.'

'I've got the details in my files. I'll get my assistant to do it,' said Brad.

'Right. I have to get back to her. Wait here until we call you. It shouldn't be long.'

She pushed her way through the swing door and disappeared down a long passageway. Brad seemed thunderstruck.

'I didn't know she was fragile,' he said. 'I didn't mean to, well, you know. She can't have...'

I caught his drift. I did not feel sympathetic as he had bullied Freya ruthlessly. However, she didn't seem too bothered the last time I saw her. She had her secret project and radiated contentment. While Brad sent a text to his PA asking for the contact details of Freya's parents, I sent a text to Harry. He called me back immediately. I took the phone outside into the freezing wind and realised I had left my coat behind.

'What's going on?' he said. 'I came to meet you at Second Home and they told me you'd gone to the hospital with Brad.'

'A cast member was taken ill, and they rushed her to the hospital. I can't elaborate right now. Brad asked me to come along and explain the protocols in British hospitals.'

'Is there anything I can do?'

'I forgot my coat and I'm freezing. Can you please bring it to me? I'll be finished soon and we can drive home together.'

'Okay. I'm helping Ghita move some furniture around. I'll come when I've finished. Are you at A and E?'

'Yes.'

'Stay put. I'll be there soon.'

When I went back inside, Brad had approached the reception desk and was waving his credit card at the startled receptionist. She called me over.

'Can you please take this man away? He's not listening to me.'

Brad turned to me.

'She won't take my card. Don't they accept American Express in your country?'

'Not in hospitals. Why don't you sit down?'

'But Freya is in trouble. I feel responsible, but this person won't let me pay.'

'You need to listen. We have a national health service in Great Britain, paid for by our taxes. Health care is free.'

'But what about the medicines?'

'It's all taken care of by the government. I think you have Medicare in the States, which is similar.'

'Yes, but there's a deductible. It can be enormous.'

'There are no deductibles here unless you count the massive taxes we pay. I suppose we pay in advance.'

'For something you might not use.'

'Yes, but if you get ill, it's all covered, always.'

'So, Freya is covered.'

'Absolutely.'

He sunk into a chair and mopped his brow with his sleeve. I patted him on the arm.

'Calm down. They're doing everything they can.'

A harried nurse came through the doors and headed for us. A shiver ran up my spine when I noticed her manner.

'Can you come with me if you want to see Miss Watson?'

'Of course,' said Brad, but the receptionist held up her hand.

'Do you have the details for her next of kin yet?'

'Can I give them to you later?' said Brad.

'I'd prefer them straight away.'

Brad scrolled through his phone, waving me away.

'I'll be there in a minute,' he said. 'My PA hasn't got back to me yet. I have to call her.'

I followed the nurse through the swinging doors and down the corridor. We rose in the lift to the second floor where we entered a ward with eight beds, four on each side. The fluorescent lights flickered above them throwing long shadows. Curtains surrounded the bed nearest the window and I couldn't see inside them.

'She's in there,' said the nurse. 'I'm afraid you won't get much from her. She's seriously ill. I don't think she'll last the hour.'

'What's wrong with her?'

'We can't be certain, but it appears to be an overdose. Was she suicidal?'

'I don't think so.'

'Well, I'll leave you to it. I hope her parents live nearby.'

She shuffled off.

Freya had been hooked up to a heart monitor and a drip, and purple bruises surrounded the needles inserted into the veins at the crook of her elbow. I felt slightly sick at the sight. I've never been great with needles. She lay on her back with her black curls spread out on the pillow and her rosebud lips dry, but still dark red. When I first met her, I only noticed her puffy face, but now I realised how beautiful she was. She resembled Sleeping Beauty lying there, deathly pale, waiting for her prince to come.

I took her hand as gently as I could and rubbed her palm with my thumb. To my surprise, what appeared to be a smile twisted her lips.

'What did you do?' I whispered. 'We can save you. Tell me.'

Her lips moved, but no sound came out. A gurgle issued from her throat and her eyes opened and rolled back. An alarm issued from the heart monitor. I let go of her hand and searched frantically for somebody to help her. Two tall skinny nurses came running towards me and shooed me away.

'Wait downstairs,' said one.

'Take him with you,' said the other.

Brad had entered the room, and he hovered in the doorway, pale with shock. The alarm squealed in the silent ward. I grabbed his arm.

'We must go downstairs again,' I said. 'We'll be in the way here.'

'But—'

'Come on,' I said, tugging his sleeve.

Tears ran down my cheeks as we stood in the lift. Brad dabbed at them with a piece of hand towel. His cheek muscles worked, but he did not speak. We entered the reception and sat down again.

'Everything all right up there?' asked the receptionist.

I shook my head unable to speak. She bit her lip and avoided my eyes. Brad took out a tiny silver crucifix he had on a chain around his neck. He rubbed it between his thumb and forefinger and muttered. From his tone of voice, I suspected him of wishing harm on someone. I wished Harry would appear. I felt lost. What had Freya tried to tell me?

A nurse pushed her way through the door into the waiting area. I knew Freya had died before she said anything. Brad slumped in his chair when she shook her head.

'Oh my God,' he said. 'What am I going to do? Can I speak to the manager, please?'

'The manager?'

'Whoever's in charge here. Nobody must know about Freya Watson's death. It must be kept secret until we can release the news. Please advise the nurses they must pretend Freya is in a coma until an official announcement of her death.'

I guess when you're a narcissist, even people dying only matters because of how it will affect you. The doors to the entrance opened and Harry came in with my coat. I threw myself into his arms, sobbing.

'What happened?' he said.

'Freya's dead. She killed herself,' said Brad, before I could answer. 'Silly cow.'

Luckily, Harry held me tight, which prevented me from punching Brad in the face.

'Get me out of here, please,' I said, sniffling into his chest.

'What about me?' said Brad.

'I think you should wait for Freya's parents. After all, you handle her as the producer of the show,' I said. 'Anyway, don't you have to talk to the manager of the hospital?'

'Aren't you going to wait with me?' said Brad.

'She's had a horrible shock. I'm taking her home,' said Harry, puffing out his chest.

Brad assessed Harry and knew when he was beaten.

'I'll wait here then,' he said. 'I'm sure someone will come and get me if I call them. Whatever you do, please don't tell anyone Freya has died.'

'But what will I say?'

'Pretend she is in a coma for now. I need to speak to her parents and get permission while we keep the press at bay.'

I was so shocked I couldn't think of any objection. I nodded and left with Harry. As we walked across the car park, I turned to him.

'This is not right,' I said. 'Freya Watson did not kill herself.'

'How do you know?'

'She told me she would soon quit the show as she had a fantastic project lined up. She was super excited about it. Can we go straight to the police station? George should send a team to the hotel before any evidence disappears. And Flo should do an autopsy.'

He held my shoulders in his warm hands and stared deep into my eyes.

'Are you sure?'

'I'm afraid so. Killing herself now makes little sense. I think Freya's plan may have got her murdered.'

Chapter 11

To give George his due, he came straight out to the front lobby when I turned up at Seacastle police station and asked to see him. He only rolled his eyes once when I told him about Freya Watson's death and the need for confidentiality.

'Can you treat it as a suspicious poisoning without letting people know she has died?' I asked.

'Possibly. Why do you think it's a murder?'

I explained my theory to him. He didn't approve of hunches, but he respected my opinion. He rubbed his chin and sighed. His keen observation skills would soon tell him if my theory had legs. He would be grumpy about me interfering, but I could deal with that. Luckily, George and I had a long history together. We were married for almost a decade and he had grown to respect my ability to see people's motives when he floundered under stacks of evidence. He had never admitted how much he depended on me, but I knew. Since we had been divorced, I had assisted him on several twisty cases and he had even paid me as a consultant once.

Mouse had tried to persuade me to become a full-time sleuth, but I didn't fancy wading through the swamps of deception and despair which were the fodder of private detectives. From what I could make out, many spent their lives sitting in old cars up to their knees in empty coffee cups and fast-food wrappers, spying on people's husbands or wives having it off with their personal assistants and gym instructors. They were then forced to tell the injured party about the dalliance and show them photographs through their storms of tears and recrimination. Being an unofficial detective meant I could investigate with a subtlety not available to them. I much preferred running my marginally profitable vintage shop and haring around the countryside with Harry. If the odd murder fell in my lap, I revelled in the investigation, but I didn't want to deal with the small stuff.

George sighed.

'Honestly, Tan. You're a worse murder magnet than that Jessica Fletcher we used to watch on telly. I don't know how you do it. Maybe you're a serial killer and you have us all fooled.'

'It's not my fault. The hospital is calling it a suicide, but I talked to her yesterday and she certainly didn't show signs of desperation. She had plans for her future, which included a secretive project which made her eyes light up. Killing herself makes little sense.'

'Could somebody from Sloane Rangers have silenced her?' said Harry. 'She might have been blackmailing people about past scandals on the show. Who knows what motive they had?'

'Okay. You've convinced me. I'll send the forensics team to Freya's hotel room and tell the hospital to keep the body for a thorough autopsy. All our teams will be instructed to keep her death confidential for now. Tan, will you come with me? I'll secure the Cavendish for examination by the forensic team. The cast and crew recognise you, so they'll find it easier to trust me if you come along.'

I turned to Harry, who nodded.

'That makes sense,' he said. 'Are you feeling up to it? I know it's been a terrible shock for you.'

I wanted to go home. I couldn't think of anything worse than returning to the Cavendish. But I sighed and said 'okay'.

'I'll drop her home to you after we get the forensics team set up,' said George.

'Good. I'll get something in the oven. I'm sure you're starving,' said Harry.

My stomach growled, and we all laughed.

'So that's a yes,' I said. 'Thanks. See you back at the house.'

'Look after her,' said Harry to George.

'Always.'

A lump rose in my throat. Sometimes you get lucky and sometimes your luck is doubled. I was proud of my good relationship with George, and he loved Harry in his own macho way, so we made the best of our situation. George broke the spell by grabbing my arm.

'Don't get all sentimental on me. We've got work to do. Follow me and we'll pick up a squad car at the back of the office.'

I blew Harry a kiss, and we passed through the security doors into the main body of the police station. I got some curious glances from the old stagers as I walked through with my ex-husband. George used to get a ribbing about me from his team, but a lot less since he and Helen had become an item. Nobody knew what to make of it. When asked, I claimed to be content, which trumped being miserable, but we weren't the most conventional extended family in England.

We found DS Joe Brennan, George's right arm, loitering in the forensic lab with Flo Barrington, the consultant forensic pathologist. He had a serious interest in the subject and Flo loved to pass on her knowledge. Flo and I were relatively close, and she had been corresponding with Harry's brother Nick since a rather jolly Christmas together. She lifted her head from her desk as we entered, her long hair piled on her head in a haphazard bun. She raised an eyebrow when she saw me behind George, and I gave her a cheeky grin.

'I've got an autopsy for you at the hospital,' said George. 'Can you call them and arrange it, please? The deceased is named Freya Watson. They need to extract her with the utmost secrecy. She is not officially dead yet.'

Flo's jaw dropped, and she blinked rapidly.

'But isn't she a member of the cast of Sloane Rangers? She's only a young woman. Don't tell me she overdosed on something.'

'They're calling it a potential suicide, but Typhoid Mary here thinks she may have been helped off the mortal coil.'

I could see Flo struggling not to explain who Typhoid Mary was, while coping with my revelation. In the end, she picked up the phone.

'Right on it, boss,' she said.

Joe Brennan followed us as we headed for the car lot at the back of the station. George's saloon car was the only vehicle available, so we jumped into it and headed for the Cavendish. Joe Brennan did not watch Sloane Rangers, but he had heard of Freya Watson. He whistled and scratched his head.

'Blimey. I bet that show's a right can of worms,' he said. 'Everybody sleeping with everybody else, lots of coke and drink in the rooms, jealousies, rivalries and what not.'

George cleared his throat.

'Can we drop the speculation please? This is an enquiry into an unexplained death, not a TV show. I'll expect you to behave professionally in there. No autographs.'

'Of course, boss. I wouldn't dream of it. There's only us in the car. I was having a bit of fun.'

'Right. Okay, as long as you understand. She is in a coma, not dead. Please don't let anyone know the truth.'

I felt sorry for Joe. George could be tough on the young man, but it was mostly because he had groomed him for high rank since spotting his potential early in Joe's career. He was somewhat of a surrogate son when Mouse had gone AWOL for a couple of years, disappointing and alienating George. Joe had passed his DS exams with flying colours and George worried he would soon lose him to a more glamorous beat like London or Birmingham.

We pulled up outside the hotel and I noticed the Vardy brothers standing on the steps smoking. They sneered at me as we walked past. I hadn't yet distinguished one from the other, but Joe would figure it out. He had a keen eye for people's tics. As we entered the lobby, I noticed Brad had arrived back at the hotel. He had commandeered a few large couches and arranged them in a square, thus acting as a barrier to entry for anyone not a member of the Sloane Rangers cast. Daisy and Zak sat together on one couch with Natasha Golova. Zak's face was white with stress and misery. He didn't appear to notice our arrival. Milly and Rose sat with Ollie Matthews; their faces blotchy from crying. Brad sat with Hugo and Carrie, and the other couch was empty. The Vardys had probably occupied it before they left for a smoke.

George planted himself at the corner formed by two of the couches and took out his warrant card.

'I'm DI George Carter and this is DS Joe Brennan. We're here to investigate the unexplained illness of Freya Watson.'

Brad jumped up to confront him.

'Now, one darn minute here. Freya tried to kill herself. Isn't that what the hospital told us, Tanya?'

'I'm afraid it's not a certainty,' said George. 'Freya Watson was a healthy young woman with no history of mental health issues, unless I hear otherwise. And under British law, we are required to investigate any unexplained illness to ensure foul play can be excluded as a cause for it.'

'Foul play?' said Milly. 'What do you mean?'

'That somebody has poisoned her on purpose,' said George.

'And who are you?' said Joe, taking out his phone and making notes on it with a stylus.

'I'm Milly Ponsonby and this is Rose Hart and Ollie Matthews.'

Joe gestured at Brad.

'I'm Brad Fordham, the producer of Sloane Rangers, and these two are Hugo and Carrie. They were not in Seacastle today, so you can probably eliminate them from your enquiries.'

'I'll decide who gets eliminated,' said George, drawing his brows together.

'We went on a day trip to Brighton to visit the Pavilion,' said Hugo.

'It is amazing,' said Carrie. 'All those dragons. I...'

She trailed off when she saw George's face. Daisy half rose from the couch to face George and Joe.

'And I'm Daisy Kallis and this is Zak Kenton. I found Freya in her room and called an ambulance.'

'And you are?' said Joe, gesturing at Natasha who had retreated behind a pillar.

She sighed.

'Natasha Golova. I'm the health and safety officer. I run the staff clinic.'

'Where are you from?' said George.

'Russia originally, but I've been in Britain for years. I used to work on "Uncovering the Truth" with Tanya.'

'Is everyone present?' said Joe.

'Of course not,' said Brad. 'The technical crew is missing.'

'And where are they?' said George.

'They're staying in the Premier Inn on Marine Drive.'

'We'll have to interview them tomorrow. Can you please contact them and ask them to stay put until we get there, Mr Fordham?' said Joe.

'It's Brad. I'll do that now.'

'I'll need to record the layout upstairs,' said Joe. 'Is there a map somewhere?'

'There's a map showing the fire escapes at reception. You could take a photograph of it,' said Ollie.

'Can you show me where everyone's rooms are, so I can tag them on the photograph?' said Joe.

'I have a list,' said Natasha. 'I'm in charge of everyone's welfare so I need to know where they are. I'll make you a copy.'

'At all times,' drawled a voice behind me. Aeneas and Hector had come in from their cigarette break.

'I'm Aeneas Vardy, and this is my brother Hector.'

'He's lying,' said Ollie. 'He's Hector. You can tell from the scar above his eyebrow.'

Joe narrowed his eyes.

'Thank you, Ollie, wasn't it? I'll soon sort them out.'

'Natasha, can you please lead us upstairs with Daisy and show us where Freya was found? Joe, can you take statements down here?' said George.

'Right oh,' said Joe. 'I'll start with the Vardy twins.'

A groan greeted this statement, but he ignored it. George pursed his lips.

'I hope it's obvious,' he said. 'But don't leave the hotel again without permission from one of us. The forensics team will be here soon. Please cooperate with them in every way and don't clean your rooms. Touch nothing, move nothing and preferably stay downstairs until you get the all clear.'

'Where are we going to sleep?' said Aeneas Vardy, crimson with fury.

'I'll talk to management,' said Brad. 'It's low season here, so the hotel is nowhere near full. We can move to different rooms for tonight if you want the top floor kept clear.'

'That would be fantastic,' said George. 'Thanks a lot. Miss Golova, if you would be so kind?'

Chapter 12

We squeezed into the lift, and Natasha pressed the button for the top floor. A plaque on the wall of the lift gave its capacity as six people, but we were pressed together in uncomfortable proximity. I could smell the damp odour rising from George's tweed suit. He never used an umbrella as he had this weird idea about them being unmasculine. Daisy's perfume mixed in with the damp smell. It was like being surrounded by a honeysuckle hedge. I noticed the tight line of Natasha's lips and her white knuckles where she gripped onto her list. Did she know something about Freya's death?

'Can we check Freya's room first?' said George.

'It's down here,' said Daisy, leading us along the corridor.

'Please don't enter the room or touch the doorframe,' said George.

'But I've already been in here.'

'Please do as I say. How can we open the door?'

'I have a passkey for all the doors,' said Natasha. 'Just in case.'

This struck me as strange. In case what? She held it up to the lock, and it clicked open. George pushed the door with his foot and held it ajar. He cleared his throat and put out his arm to stop Daisy from walking in.

'Wait at the door, please. Tan, can you take notes for me?'

He entered the room and stood like a statue, taking in the scene. The double bed with its tattered pink counterpane. The cheap bedside tables with their wonky drawers. The sealed windows splattered with seagull excrement. Then he searched the room patiently, moving from surface to surface. I removed my notebook and pen from my handbag and waited while he searched, lifting things with the end of a pencil. The pillow still held the imprint of Freya's head and I could make out a stray black hair draped across it. Poor Freya.

'Did you find a suicide note?' asked George, making us jump.

'She didn't leave one, as far as I know,' said Daisy. 'I mean, why would I look? I found her unconscious and went to get Natasha. We thought she was ill.'

'And what did you do, Miss Golova?'

'I examined Freya and took her pulse. It was dangerously slow, so I called an ambulance immediately.'

She glanced at me for validation.

'Were there any pill bottles in Freya's room?' said George

'No. Not that I saw,' she said, wringing her hands. 'I didn't realise, I thought...'

'What did you think?' asked George.

Natasha looked at her feet and sighed.

'I thought she might be having a reaction to her medicine.'

'What was she taking? Was she an epileptic?'

'No. She had been injecting Ozempic to lose weight. I wondered if she had tried to speed up her weight loss by injecting a larger dose.'

'Why would she do that?'

'Brad was pressuring her,' I said. 'All the girls on the cast are injecting Ozempic.'

George's jaw worked, but he failed to speak.

'It's not dangerous,' said Natasha. 'If you follow the dosage instructions. I keep the syringes in my fridge so I can monitor people's intake. She couldn't have taken an extra dose without me knowing about it.'

'You'd better show me where you keep the medicines,' said George.

'The medical room is over there,' said Natasha. 'I keep it locked.'

We followed her the short distance to her clinic, and she opened the door with her pass key. George whistled when he saw the set up.

'Are you a qualified medic?' he said.

'Yes. I'm a nurse,' said Natasha.

'What's in the fridge?'

'That's where we keep the Ozempic.'

George pulled the door open and peered in, the light making him look like a gargoyle. He did a double take when he noticed the number of boxes.

'How on earth do you keep track of whose is whose?'

'I have a list which contains the names and dosages of everyone who is using it. Each box is labelled with the person's name taking that dosage.'

'Who decides which dose people should take?'

'There's a system,' said Natasha. 'The weekly dose starts at a minimum amount and increases every four weeks when the pen is empty. After that, the patient decides if they graduate to a higher dose.'

'How so?' asked George.

'Some people find the side effects become unbearable at higher doses.'

'What do they do then?'

'They stay on a lower dose.'

'If someone injected too much Ozempic, would that send them into a coma?'

'I don't know. I don't think so.'

'What about heavy sweating?'

'That isn't one of the known side effects.'

'And what are they?'

'Nausea, vomiting, diarrhoea, stomach pain, low blood sugar.'

'When did Freya have her last injection?'

Natasha avoided his inquiring glance.

'She came in after lunch.'

'This afternoon? Did you supervise her?'

'Of course. I monitor everyone. They can't get into the clinic without me being present.'

George rubbed his chin. He pulled a plastic bag from a roll and gave one to Natasha.

'Please place the Ozempic boxes in this bag with your list of the names and dosages. What do those small bottles contain?'

'You can't take those. They are antibiotics. We might need them if someone contracts an infection.'

'Okay. Leave them there for now. The forensic team will do an inventory later. You need to keep the clinic shut for now,' said George.

'Brad won't be happy. Ozempic is expensive.'

George swore under his breath.

'A young woman is in a coma. I don't care how upsct he is.'

He held out his hand for the now full bag and sealed it.

'I'll send someone from forensics downstairs when they arrive to take everyone's fingerprints for elimination.'

A loud ping broke the silence. The forensic team stepped out of the lift already suited up for work. They came towards us carrying their equipment.

'Can you lend them the pass key please?' said George.

Natasha sighed theatrically, but she handed it over.

'Right. I'll stay here and explain what we need. Can you ladies please go back to the lobby and wait for fingerprinting there?'

Natasha lasted until the lift doors closed before bursting into tears.

'Don't cry,' said Daisy. 'It's not your fault.'

'But what if they deport me? I don't want to return to Russia.'

'As long as you didn't cause Freya's coma, you'll be fine,' I said. 'George is not interested in your immigration status. He is laser focused when he is investigating a serious crime.'

'A crime? But Brad told us it was a suicide attempt,' said Daisy.

'Brad wanting it to be a suicide doesn't make it one. Perhaps forensics will find evidence either way.'

'Can we see her?'

'She's in a deep coma. The hospital is not letting anyone visit for now. If they change their mind, they'll let us know.'

Chapter 13

We emerged from the lift to find the cast still gathered together. Someone had ordered drinks and an ice bucket sat on the coffee table at the centre of the couches, dripping condensation on the marble surface. Aeneas and Hector Vardy conversed with Joe, who had figured them out pretty quickly. They were talking about rugby and braying with laughter at some quip he made about Joe Marler. Natasha and Daisy returned to their places beside Zak. He had dropped his head in his hands, but when Daisy sat beside him, he approached me.

'Did you find anything?' he said.

'Oh, I didn't look. That's my ex-husband's job.'

A shadow of a smile crossed his face.

'Are you sure you're not in a competing reality show? Your story board must make fascinating reading.'

'We are not a very conventional bunch, but we all get along.'

'Unlike us? I suppose that's fair. Freya's coma is genuine enough, though.'

His hand flew to his forehead.

'She is ill, isn't she? I wouldn't put it past Brad to pull a fast one on us. Everyone is paranoid since he took over the production. We don't know which way is up.'

'Unfortunately, it's not a nightmare, or one of Brad's plot twists. She's at the hospital right now.'

'Will they carry out tests for poison?'

'It's the only way to discover what happened to her.'

'How dreadful. I knew the series was on its last legs, but I never imagined this.'

He shook his head.

'Surely you don't think this is a ploy to revive it?'

'I don't know what I think. Daisy won't speak to me because of some stupid rumour about Freya, and now Freya may have been poisoned. It's an awful mess.'

'Would you talk to me about the series?' I asked. 'I need to understand the relationship dynamics better, and you're the longest serving member of the cast.'

'Are you spying for George?'

'Sort of. Don't you want to find out who tried to poison Freya?'

'If she was poisoned.'

'If one of the show's cast or crew did it.'

'Okay. It can't do any harm. This show is dead anyway.'

The lift doors opened and George came out, pulling on his jacket.

'Ah, there you are, Tan. I'll give you and Daisy a lift home, shall I?'

When George had dropped Joe Brennan off at the station, he took us back to Keat's Road. Daisy sat in the back seat without speaking, her head bowed. We got out together, and George leaned towards me across the passenger seat.

'Since Brad has cancelled filming tomorrow, while he speaks to the show's backers, I'd like you to come to the station for a debrief. Can you arrive at eleven o'clock?'

I nodded.

'Sure. I'll be there.'

When George drove off, I turned to find Daisy standing forlornly on the pavement. She seemed lost. I pressed the doorbell of Gladys's house for her.

'Get some rest,' I said. 'You'll be suffering from shock after what happened today.'

The door opened, and Gladys came out. Her smile vanished as she took in Daisy's collapsed state.

'Oh my, what has happened to our girl?'

'A member of the cast ended up in the hospital today. She's in a coma, and they've been sent home until further notice.'

'That's terrible. Who is it?'

'Freya Watson.'

'But she's only a young woman. Was it an overdose?'

'We don't know yet. George has got involved because it may be a poisoning.'

'How heart wrenching. I'm so sorry. Don't worry. I'll look after Daisy.'

'Are you sure? I feel responsible for her being in your house.'

Gladys pursed her lips.

'I'm perfectly capable of dealing with loss. I'm an expert.'

She put an arm around Daisy's shoulders and shepherded her inside. I shrugged and let myself in to our house. Harry rushed forward and enveloped me in a warm throw. He let me sit on the sofa while he made me a hot chocolate 'for the shock'. I felt my stress ebb away as Hades allowed me a micro snuggle before stalking out through the cat flap.

'You've had a rough day,' said Harry.

'Appalling.'

'Do you want to talk about it?'

'Is it okay if we don't? I'm drained by the whole affair. I'd like to get into bed and pretend it didn't happen.'

'It's only seven-thirty.'

'So?'

'Okay, go up and put on your PJs. I'll bring you a bowl of beef casserole to eat in bed.'

'Can I have a hot water bottle?'

'I'll eat my supper first, and then you can have a human one. I don't mind an early night. That book I'm reading is brilliant.'

Soon I was ensconced in bed, trying to gobble down the delicious casserole Harry had cooked without scalding my throat. He had recently started to cook our supper sometimes, a talent he had kept hidden until then. I suspect his army buddies had teased him about it; enough to stop him from trying. He came home one day with his deceased wife's recipe book, which he had been keeping in storage, and put it on the shelf in the kitchen next to mine. That seemingly insignificant gesture brought us closer than ever. And Cathy knew her onions. What delicious food we made from those recipes! I liked to think she would have approved of Harry being happy again.

Despite not wanting to talk about Freya's death, I couldn't get it out of my head. I felt compelled to review the notes I had taken for George, but nothing jumped out at me from them.

Harry entered the bedroom and put his hands on his hips when he saw me gazing at my notebook.

'Honestly. I thought you didn't want to talk about it.'

'I don't. I didn't. Well, maybe a little. Your casserole has restored me to working order.'

He tried to hide a smile.

'Heaven help us,' he said. 'Go on. Tell me what you're thinking or you'll never be able to sleep.'

'I can't believe Freya killed herself. She had her whole life planned out, including a secret project, which made her extremely excited. George agrees with me.'

'It seems like a strange decision. Are you sure nothing happened to her to make her lose hope? Maybe Zak dumped her, or the project got cancelled.'

'From what I saw, she was ruled by her emotions, but I hadn't talked to her today, so it's possible something, or someone, upset her.'

'Well, nobody kills without a motive. I'm sure you can find out what happened if you carry out your usual magic on the suspects. However, I don't think we should dwell on it now. You need to ask questions first.'

'I can't go to sleep now. It's way too early.'

'I've got a few good ideas.'

Chapter 14

The next morning, I had planned to go to Second Home and update the accounts, but my reluctance to carry out this onerous task made me procrastinate at home. When Daisy knocked on my front door, I took it as a sign and welcomed her in. She had dark bags under her brown eyes and her dirty blonde hair had been twisted into a makeshift plait.

'Hi Tanya. I hope I'm not disturbing you.'

'Not at all. Do you want a lift somewhere? I'm off to the shop shortly.'

'I hoped we might talk. About Freya.'

'Freya?'

'Brad told us you were with her in the hospital. And I wondered...'

She tailed off, and I took pity on her.

'Come in for a minute?' I said, my mind racing.

She slipped past me and headed for the couch. Hades looked up in disgust and dashed to the cat flap, leaving her with an outstretched hand, which she quickly lowered.

'Do you want a cup of tea or coffee? I'm afraid we only have instant. It's one of the good ones, though.'

'Um, no thanks. Gladys pumps me full of tea at all hours of the day and night. I'm about to spring a leak.'

I sat opposite her on one of the scruffy armchairs, suddenly self-conscious about the ramshackle furnishings in the Grotty Hovel. She gazed around the room.

'It's so cosy in here,' she said. 'My house looked like a showroom.'

'Thank you. I thought it was extraordinary. Zak had some fabulous pieces.'

'Where are they now?'

'Harry is keeping them in storage. We haven't had time to value them yet. I'll probably sell some of them to my friend Grace. She owns a high-end antique shop at the other end of the high street to mine.'

'Look. I should've told you before, but I'd prefer if you didn't sell them until we've left Seacastle. Is that okay?'

'Of course. If that's what you want.'

She frowned.

'Zak might get violent if he sees his stuff for sale.'

'You haven't told him about it yet?'

'No. I haven't had a chance to talk to him. He stayed up in London until the last minute before he came to Seacastle. He was discussing some project. That's what he told me, but maybe he hung out with Freya.'

'Talking of Freya, what did you want to ask me about her?'

'Freya? Oh yes. Did she say anything to you?'

'About what?'

'I mean, did she speak to you in the hospital? Maybe she gave you a message for Zak?'

'No, she didn't. She had already fallen into a coma by the time we reached the hospital and she didn't wake up while I was there.'

'Do you think she was poisoned?'

'Why would anyone poison Freya? She seems pretty harmless.'

Daisy snorted.

'I thought that. Until she stole Zak.'

'But didn't you break up with him?'

She shrugged.

'I don't know what's real anymore. Is Freya really in a coma? Did Zak punch me? Was it all in the script? I'm not sure about real life anymore. Starring in a reality show is like living in another dimension. If you do it too long, you don't know where you belong.'

Her misery was genuine enough. She appeared lost and confused. A girl with ten million followers and no friends. I leaned across and patted her arm.

'How are your selling skills?'

'My what?'

'Do you want to hang out at Second Home? I need to meet my ex-husband at the police station soon, but I'll be back afterwards. We can drink proper coffee and eat a slice of one of Ghita's fabulous cakes.'

'I'd like that. Shall we walk?'

'I think we'll go in the car. I need to visit the supermarket later and stock up on cat food.'

'What's the name of your cat?'

'Hades. He's not the friendliest. He's quite picky. I had to wait a year for him to sit on my lap.'

'I don't think he liked me. I'll get my coat.'

The heavens opened while we were driving to Second Home, so we sat in the Mini, waiting for the deluge to subside. I noticed Daisy had chewed her nails to the quick. I wondered if Harry had been right about her weight.

'Um, Freya told me all the girls on the show were prescribed Ozempic. Is that true?'

'Yes, even me. Now I weigh less than a wet cat. My fingers look like spaghettis. If the series doesn't end soon, I might disappear.'

'Why don't you stop? It's not like you need to lose weight.'

'Natasha will get in trouble with Brad if I stop.'

'Can you still eat cake?'

'Try to stop me.'

The rain eased off, and we made a dash for the shop. Daisy ran headlong into Ghita whose look of astonishment, as she fell on her bottom, made me crease up with laughter.

'We're making a habit of bumping into Daisy Kallis,' I said, pulling Ghita off the floor.

'I'm so sorry,' said Ghita. 'I can't believe it.'

Daisy grinned.

'You didn't bump into me. I careered into you. It was entirely my fault. I should apologise, not you.'

Roz came bounding downstairs and enveloped Daisy in a hug.

'I'm Roz,' she said. 'And you're welcome to Second Home. Did Tanya bribe you to come and see us?'

'No, I didn't. Daisy's taken the day off and she didn't want to hang out at Gladys's house. I thought she could stay here and chat while I meet George.'

Roz slapped her forehead.

'I'm so stupid. It's about Freya Watson, isn't it? My second cousin works in the hospital as a porter and he told me —- Ow!'

I kicked her hard and shook my head.

'She's in a coma,' I said. 'It's being kept quiet for now, Roz. Please don't talk about it.'

Trust Roz to have a cousin in the hospital. She had relatives all over Seacastle who fed her every scrap of gossip.

'Freya Watson in a coma?' said Ghita. 'What happened?'

'We don't know yet, but it isn't common knowledge so please don't tell anybody about it.'

Roz rolled her eyes.

'Honestly. It's the best piece of gossip I've had since I saw my neighbour's wife bonking the postman in the garden shed. You can't expect me to keep it a secret.'

She caught the sharp look I threw at her.

'Oh. You do. Okay, but for how long?'

'Yes, I do and so does George. Please keep it quiet until it's official. The national press will be all over this news like a rash. Can you imagine what would happen if it turns out to be deliberate?'

Even as I said it, I remembered my promise to Jim Swift. It would not be ethical to tell him yet, but I owed him a heads up of the announcement's date. I grinned as I imagined his excitement. He loved a scoop.

'Don't worry. We'll look after her,' said Ghita. 'In fact, I'm about to make a cake at Surfusion. Do you want to help?'

'You bake? Oh, yes, please. Do you mind, Roz?'

Roz sighed.

'I'll be fine. It's not like the shop is flooded with customers.'

Ghita and Daisy ran giggling through the rain to Surfusion and disappeared into the restaurant.

I patted Roz on the shoulder.

'Thanks. I won't be long. I'm sorry about the kick. None of the cast members know Freya died yet. It's important to keep it a secret for now. I promise to tell you all about it when I get back.'

Roz's eyes lit up with excitement.

'Really?'

'Everything I can, but only you. I don't want Daisy to know the details until George takes her off his suspect list.'

'Daisy Kallis is a suspect? I thought it was a suicide.'

'It's an unexplained death right now. And you know George. Everyone's a suspect until he says so.'

'I can't wait.'

Chapter 15

I took my umbrella from the shop and trudged along the High Street to the police station. Beads of water sat on the toes of my boots, making me glad I had waterproofed them the week before. The uneven pavements collected muddy water in puddles, some deeper than they looked. I saw one poor woman get a soggy foot after misjudging the depth of one. She let fly with a few choice swear words as she hopped about. We were almost alone on the street. Everyone had retreated into the cafes to wait out the rain. I mounted the steps to the police station and entered the small, sweltering reception area. I don't know why they kept it at that temperature. It would have been perfect for growing orchids: Hot, sweaty and peopled with slow-moving primates. I imagined myself turning into a sloth or a bushbaby if I stayed too long. Sally Wright, the receptionist, grinned at me as I squelched into the station.

'Nice weather for ducks?' she said. 'He's ready for you. I can buzz you through if you like.'

'Thanks.'

I pushed my way through the security doors and headed for the interview room. I never entered George's office. It seemed like a liberty. I usually took off my shoes when entering the interview room, as I got electric shocks from the furniture. However, there was no danger of that in my soggy state. My folded umbrella dripped onto the nylon carpet under my chair, a fact noticed by George, who tutted at me.

'Honestly. Aren't there enough puddles outside? Why did you bring one in with you?'

Before I could think of a retort, Flo entered, closely followed by Joe, who carried a fat pile of folders. She sat beside George, fluffing out her taffeta skirt. I could see him stiffening as it touched his leg. He didn't like anyone in his space. Joe gave me a wink and parked himself beside me. He dropped the folders in front of him.

'I thought you were running a paperless office,' I said.

'The boss likes a written copy.'

George sniffed.

'I don't trust computers. What if there's a strong solar storm?'

Flo snorted, but covered it up well by blowing her nose.

'Shall I get started?' she said.

'Why doesn't Tanya fill us in on the background first?' said Joe. 'I'd like to understand the dynamics.'

'I've only worked on set a couple of days, but there are definitely some powerful undercurrents. The female members of the cast are seething with resentment because Brad Fordham, the new producer, has instigated a compulsory slimming regime. They are all injecting themselves with Ozempic.'

'Surely they would have murdered Brad, rather than Freya, if that was the motive?' said Flo.

'Didn't Freya inject herself yesterday before she fell into her coma?' said George.

'Yes. And she was involved in a love triangle with Zak Kenton and Daisy Kallis, which caused a massive row on set the first morning I joined them.'

'Jealousy takes over a production,' said Joe. 'The Vardy brothers were complaining about their screen time. It's a big deal.'

'I thought the Vardys were supposed to be working at a London brokerage office. Don't they earn plenty from that work already?' said George.

'Some people carry on lucrative side hustles, or are negotiating them. The Vardys think they need greater exposure to get better deals,' said Joe.

'I'd be looking at the love triangle,' said George. 'It's always the husband.'

'Freya wasn't married,' I said.

'What did you discover from her body?' said George.

'Give me a chance. Her body only came in an hour ago,' said Flo. 'I've also got the Ozempic pens to examine. I'm going to send a sample from Freya's pen to check its contents. Her symptoms were strange. Even if she injected too much Ozempic, it wouldn't have caused a coma.'

'Can't you do a test on the contents in your lab?' said George.

'Unfortunately, specialist equipment is necessary. If the syringe doesn't contain Ozempic, they will have to run a battery of tests to identify the contents.'

'You mean someone could have swapped the contents of the pen for something else?' I asked.

'That sounds like murder to me,' said Joe.

'Possibly. First, I must complete the autopsy and take samples from the injection site, because Ozempic is not dangerous, even at high doses. I'm leaning towards the contamination of her pen, whether intentional or accidental,' said Flo.

George rolled his eyes.

'I hardly think swapping the contents could be accidental. We better continue with our investigation. Did SOCO find anything interesting in the hotel rooms?'

'They haven't given me their report yet. It's early days. I think they have several rooms left to search.'

'What about Natasha Golova?' said George. 'She has a master key card. She's had sole access to the clinic and could have interfered with the Ozempic pens.'

'But what motive did she have for killing Freya?' I asked. 'Natasha is desperate to stay in Britain. She's hardly likely to risk being thrown in prison and then deported back to Russia. It doesn't make sense.'

'She claimed no-one else could enter the clinic without the pass key, but what if they did? Can you have a chat with her? I know you two used to work together. She might be more likely to tell you the truth about access. Perhaps she wasn't as scrupulous as she makes out? Maybe someone else interfered with the fridge's contents when she wasn't there?'

I nodded. He had a point. Natasha had claimed to keep the clinic locked, but I didn't remember it being shut when she bandaged my finger. Perhaps she had become careless since so many people needed to get their shots from the fridge. It was possible.

'How long before we receive the results from the lab?' said George.

'If I put a rush on, perhaps a week,' said Flo.

'And Joe, I need more background on Freya. Is there any evidence she intended to commit suicide? Obtain a warrant to search her phone records and enquire if SOCO found anything in her room which might have produced her symptoms.'

'What are you going to tell Brad? His filming schedule will be compromised if he can't restart.'

'I'll tell him he can continue to film the episodes, although how he incorporates Freya's death is a mystery.

Filming will keep everyone at Seacastle, and we can do some covert investigating until we discover if we are dealing with a murder.'

'I'll talk to Natasha as soon as I can.'

'Let me know if she comes clean about the clinic. And don't talk to Daisy if you can avoid it. Her helpless act doesn't convince me.'

I decided not to mention Zak's abusive behaviour to Daisy or his relationship with Freya until I got my facts straight. After all, Freya had died, and she hadn't been attacked by Zak. George wouldn't consider theories without evidence. And I needed more if I wanted to back up my hunches.

Chapter 16

When I got back to the shop, Roz herded me upstairs for a debrief. I couldn't reveal many details, but she gobbled up my crumbs of gossip and came to the same conclusion.

'Flo thinks it's murder too, doesn't she? Are you going to investigate?' she asked.

'I already am. Would you like to help?'

'Me? Are you joking? I'd cut my right arm off for the chance to get involved.'

'There's no need for that. Can you talk to your cousin at the hospital for me? Ask him to find out if Freya said anything to anyone before she died. She tried to tell me something, but I couldn't make it out. Perhaps she told one of the nurses? People often have a lucid moment before they die. Maybe she spoke about what happened to her?'

'I'll get right on it.'

'Discreetly.'

'Of course. You know me.'

'Yes, I do. That's why I'm telling you to be discreet. You mustn't talk to anyone about the case until it is solved.'

'I promise. But you must keep me posted on developments too.'

'I will. But don't tell Daisy anything.'

'Don't tell Daisy what?' said Ghita, coming into the shop with Daisy trailing behind her.

'It's a secret,' I said. 'Did you bring cake?'

'We've made a new flavour,' said Daisy. 'Well, Ghita did. I ate the icing with a spoon after I mixed salt into the first batch of sponges by mistake.'

Ghita rolled her eyes at me, and I stifled a snort.

'It's an orange and walnut layer cake,' said Ghita. 'It's like one of your murder mysteries. Nobody knows what's coming next.'

'Hilarious. I can't wait to try it,' I said, saliva invading my mouth.

'Isn't the décor in Surfusion amazing? I couldn't get over those spooky fish looming in the deep,' said Daisy.

Glad to stray off topic, I filled her in on the origin of the taxidermy shoal, and the Italian former owners of the restaurant, while we all had a piece of divine cake and a latte upstairs in the Vintage. Ghita had outdone herself with her delicious melt-in-the mouth orange icing. She had a habit of creating new flavour combinations for fun. I rubbed my stomach in appreciation after I finished a large slice. Daisy licked her fingers and beamed at Roz who didn't reciprocate. I guessed she was trying to stay out of any conversations where she might tell Daisy something she shouldn't. I covered the remains of the cake with a glass dome.

'This won't last long,' I said, placing it in the baked goods display cabinet. 'I wonder if you'll sell as many of these as the tipsy cherry cake you made at Christmas.'

'I'd love to,' said Ghita. 'I made a fortune. Well, lots anyway. People kept coming back for another.'

'Don't remind me,' said Roz. 'Ed scoffed almost half of ours before I could stop him.'

I left the girls to chat and went downstairs to phone Natasha. She answered immediately and agreed to talk to me in confidence away from the hotel. I got the feeling she needed to speak about the tragedy as soon as possible and I offered to see her straight away. She sighed her relief down the line. We arranged to meet immediately in the mezzanine part of the Ocean Café on the pier, where Jim Swift and I had spoken not long before.

'I'm going out for a while,' I shouted upstairs. 'I'll be back later.'

On my way to the Ocean, I received a text from Brad asking to meet him at the hotel. I gave myself an hour and a half leeway from the time of my meeting with Natasha. By the time I entered the café, I almost quivered with anticipation of what I might learn from both meetings. Despite the awful circumstances which preceded it, I found tracking down murderers very addictive. Natasha had chosen the corner table furthest from the stairway where we would not be overheard. Her white face almost shone in the gloom caused by the overcast day. She stood to give me an awkward hug, patting me up and down as if she was frisking me. I later wondered if her odd movements were an attempt to check for a wire. We all watched too many police procedurals. Then she stared into my eyes, making me feel uncomfortable.

'Are you working for the police?' she said.

'Not exactly. But I am helping them find out what happened to Freya.'

'Do they think I helped her attempt to kill herself? I know it's illegal in Britain. I had no idea she intended to do it.'

'Nobody thinks that. But we must figure out how she ended up in a coma.'

'What do you mean?'

'Well, we know she injected herself in the hours before she collapsed. Is it possible she could have injected something other than Ozempic? What about those glass vials in the fridge?'

She shook her head.

'No. They were sealed. She needed a different sort of syringe to extract the fluid. She couldn't have injected herself with something different by mistake.'

'What about on purpose?'

'Antibiotics don't put people in a coma, either. Unless you are allergic, but I presume they tested for any reactions.'

'Are you sure there wasn't anything else available in the clinic?'

She picked at her cuticle before answering.

'That would be illegal. I had bottles of household painkillers, but they were in a locked cabinet. I already checked them and none were missing after Freya got sick.'

'Could somebody have entered the clinic while you weren't there?'

'I always kept it locked.'

She wouldn't look me in the eye, but I already knew this wasn't true.

'But the door was open when I came to get my finger bandaged,' I said.

She choked and shook her head.

'How is the clinic being open connected with Freya's death? There's nothing poisonous there. Are you trying to frame me?'

She sobbed uncontrollably. I tried to put my arm around her shoulders, but she pulled away from me. I changed tack.

'Forget about the clinic for a moment. Did anyone want to harm Freya?'

She blew her nose into a large handkerchief.

'Not really. She wasn't popular, but she often heard things she shouldn't have, because people ignored her or forgot she was present. She told me once she had an eidetic memory and could recite entire conversations she had heard without forgetting a word. That made her the keeper of Sloane Rangers' secrets.'

'Could she have heard something she shouldn't and threatened to spill the beans?'

'It's possible.'

'I'm sure you know secrets about the cast members too. Is there anything you should tell me?'

'I'm a nurse. I can't reveal patients' medical details, but I have observed people's behaviour on this show. There are many rumours which would horrify their fans if they learned about them.'

'What sort of things?'

'I think the Vardy brothers are running a scam. And Ollie is pretending to be gay to stay on the show. Daisy is unhappy with Zak. And Zak received an offer from another franchise, or so I've heard. I don't know if any rumour is reality based.'

'What about Brad?'

'Brad's a complete bastard. He lies to everyone to stir the pot. He didn't like Freya at all.'

'Why?'

'You'll have to ask him. I'm going back to the hotel. I have to carry out an inventory of the clinic with a forensic officer.'

She stood up.

'Aren't you leaving?' she asked me.

'Not yet. I'm meeting someone else later, so I'll scroll through my phone and compare notes before I go.'

I watched her leave and glance back to wave at me. George would call her in eventually for an interview. I hoped she wouldn't panic. She had no motive I could fathom, but George had his method. Everyone was a suspect until motive and evidence came together. He liked to work his way through the clues. I tried to imagine being in her precarious position, living in a country where you could be thrown out at any minute. Natasha hadn't been truthful about access to her clinic, but I would try again when she felt calmer.

Chapter 17

Despite my reluctance, I girded my loins and went to the meeting with Brad. My nerves were jangling as I approached the hotel. I had not seen Brad since Harry had driven me from the hospital the day Freya died. I hoped he wouldn't remember how Harry had left him to fend for himself after he had called Freya 'a silly cow'. I tried to be generous and attribute his callous remark to his distress at her death, but I suspected his reservoir of sympathy for poor Freya was dry.

On arrival, I took the lift upstairs and went straight to Brad's room. He opened the door and pointed at the arm chairs in the window alcove without greeting me. I walked across the swirly carpet and sat down. Brad flopped into the chair opposite me; his face drawn with tiredness. He had aged ten years. He had a coffee stain on his shirt. He saw me looking at it and brushed at it without result, tutting. Then he lifted his head.

'How have you been holding up?' he said, frowning. 'I'm sorry about the way I behaved at the hospital. I must have looked like a dumbass.'

'I don't think there's a protocol for your reaction,' I said. 'I understand. You were distraught.'

'I'm glad you see it my way. Freya's death has caused a massive problem for the show, and as the producer, I'm directly responsible for our ratings. We'll make an official announcement once we draft a statement. I'm amazed the news hasn't trickled out already to tell you the truth.'

I wondered if he had any idea how self-centred he sounded. I could only imagine how his meeting with Freya's parents had gone, especially when he informed them they would have to keep quiet about their daughter's death for a few days. Actually, I doubt he informed them. He probably ordered them with some sort of vague threats about her legacy. Our relationship had not started out well and had gone downhill, but I tried to sound sympathetic.

'It has been a tough time for everyone concerned. I'm sure you'll navigate this difficulty with aplomb.'

His confused expression told me he didn't know what that meant, but I kept smiling. He scratched his head.

'I wondered if you had any news about the autopsy? Have you spoken to George yet?'

Often, but I didn't tell him that.

'The pathologist has performed the post mortem, but she's still waiting for the results from the laboratory to ascertain the cause of Freya's death.'

'Can she confirm if Freya committed suicide or not yet? What will I tell the press?'

'I think you'd be safe enough calling it an unexplained death. The press will have a field day hinting at drug overdoses and similar causes, and you can deny every rumour and accuse them of being vultures. You're bound to get lots of publicity whatever happens. I expect it will make the ratings rocket.'

He smirked at me.

'You struck me as a goody-two-shoes, but I find you pretty savvy after all. There's hope for you yet. I presume I can count on your services when I get back to Seacastle?'

I raised an eyebrow.

'You're leaving?'

'I have to meet the team in London to talk about the crisis.'

'The only services I'm offering are in our contract, by the way.'

'You know what I meant,' he said.

'I hope so. Harry can be over-protective if he misinterprets someone's motives.'

'I noticed. Don't worry. Your virtue is safe with me. I want to finish filming and leave before anyone else kicks the bucket.'

He got up, but I stayed sitting, intending to confront him.

'I heard you didn't like Freya much. Were you planning on getting rid of her?'

The blood drained from his face.

'One darn minute here. Are you accusing me of poisoning her? It's only a stupid show.'

'One you staked your reputation on. Had you heard she had planned to leave the show?'

'Leaving? Freya? Her as well? No, but I wouldn't have minded. She gave everyone the creeps. She could remember everything they said days after they said it, word for word. That's not normal. I think she had Asperger's.'

I winced at his description.

'Is somebody else leaving the show?' I asked.

'Not if I've anything to do with it. The ratings have begun to climb again. We can't afford to lose any of our stars right now.'

'But Freya dying has not affected your plans?'

'As I told you, nobody liked her, and they won't miss her. I'm sorry she's dead, but it's nothing to do with me. She must have taken an overdose of some sort. The autopsy will show I'm right.'

'When will you issue the press release about Freya's death?'

'Saturday evening. It will be front page news in all the Sunday papers, and guarantee a massive audience for this episode. We'll start filming again on Monday. Can I count on your presence?'

I couldn't leave Brad's room fast enough. When I got to the lobby, I noticed Cheryl at the reception desk and waved at her. She beckoned me over.

'Is Freya coming back soon?' she said. 'Only I've got something I need to give her.'

'Um, I'm not sure. She's in a coma, you know. Sometimes people don't recover.'

'But Seacastle hospital is fantastic. They'll save her. You'll see. Are you going to visit her?'

'I don't think so.'

'Well, if you do, can you tell her Cheryl's thinking about her?'

'Of course.'

I felt bad about lying to Cheryl, but until Brad made his announcement, Freya had not officially died yet. It occurred to me I owed Jim Swift a call. I didn't have to ask him twice. He came straight to the wind shelter on the promenade beside the theatre with a massive smile on his face. He sat beside me, shivering in his anorak, his fingers over the keyboard of his iPad.

'Couldn't we have met somewhere warmer? This venue reminds me of a spy thriller. I can tell by your face you've got a scoop for me. I'm all ears.'

'Did you hear that Freya Watson ended up in the hospital?'

'Yes, but I couldn't get past the wall of silence about why they admitted her. Normally somebody will leak the information, but, for some reason, they wouldn't talk this time.'

I moistened my lips.

'This information is top secret. It's off the record until an official announcement is made.'

'Tell me.'

'Freya Watson is dead.'

Jim gasped.

'I don't believe it. How?'

'We don't have a cause yet. The pathologist will have the results shortly, and they will confirm if it's a suicide or something more sinister. Roz has a contact in the hospital who was present when Freya was dying.'

'Something more sinister?' He looked into my eyes. 'You think someone murdered her, don't you? Oh my goodness, this could be huge.'

'It hasn't been confirmed yet. You need to be careful.'

'Don't you worry. I can look after myself. I'll track down Roz.'

'Whatever you do, only talk to her alone. I don't want anyone else finding out what we are doing. Is that clear?'

'Crystal. When can I publish?'

'An official announcement will be issued on Saturday night. The minute it surfaces, you can publish your article, so get a head start on all the other papers and research like mad.'

'Thanks, Tan. I owe you one.'

'I've a feeling you might be called into action again, if you're game.'

'Say the word.'

Chapter 18

I arrived at the shop to find Daisy waiting for me. I had forgotten I owed her a lift home. She had settled into the routine of shop life with great ease. We had more customers than usual once people realised who she was. The novelty of having Daisy Kallis serve them a coffee definitely hit the spot. That and Ghita's new cakes, which were leaving the café faster than she could bake them. As I packed up, Harry whistled his way into the shop; always a good sign. He put his arm around my waist and drew me close to him, sniffing my neck and giving me soft kisses in the dip behind my clavicle. I giggled and pushed him away, but not too hard.

'I've got news,' he said. 'I've organised the clearance of a house west of Chichester. It'll give you a chance to see Mouse.'

I squeaked with excitement.

'Really? When?'

'Tomorrow. I know you're pining.'

I kissed him tenderly.

'Oi, get a room,' said Roz.

'Can I come?' said Daisy. 'I'd love to meet Mouse. I've heard so much about him. Gladys says he's a hacker.'

'Gladys is exaggerating,' I said. 'I'm not sure—'

But Harry made a face at me.

'We'd love you to come,' he said. 'Mouse will be thrilled. You're his absolute favourite. He never misses a show.'

'But you mustn't tell him about Freya being ill,' I said. 'I don't want him worrying. He's a sensitive young man.'

'He's almost twenty and has spent the last year or two helping you solve murders. I don't think he'll be fazed by a drug overdose,' said Harry.

'I won't mention it. I promise,' said Daisy.

'We normally have a bacon sandwich before we set out and feed the crusts to Herbert. It's a tradition.'

'Who's Herbert?' said Daisy.

'You'll find out,' I said. 'He's a handsome young man too.'

I tried not to mind about Daisy coming along as I knew Mouse would be thrilled to meet her, but I couldn't help feeling a little jealous. I saw Mouse so rarely since he had started his course in forensic computing at Portsmouth. I really didn't feel like sharing him. But Harry was right as usual. Mouse had a huge crush on Daisy. If he took a couple of selfies with her, it would make his day. His fellow students would be green with envy. I pretended to be as thrilled as her and made three bacon sandwiches the next morning so she wouldn't miss out.

We rose at first light to sit in the wind shelter and drink a cup of tea with our bacon butties. Daisy nibbled at hers and made exaggerated swallowing motions as if every mouthful might choke her. I rolled my eyes inwardly and pretended I hadn't noticed. Herbert did not deign to appear, but he often stayed away in the winter. I always imagined him snuggled up with his missus in their cosy nest. Harry did not notice Daisy's struggles and jumped up as soon as he'd stuffed the last crust into his mouth.

'Driver's rules. Let's go.'

Daisy shrugged and threw her sandwich into the pebble bank. I felt guilty for enjoying her difficulties. How could I feel jealous of such a lovely person? She had suffered a horrible trauma at work, which would magnify when news of Freya's death surfaced in the press. I grinned at her.

'Sorry about the weird English customs.'

She grinned back.

'I've never understood people who spend their lives complaining about the weather, then sit outside in a gale and call it bracing.'

'We can be rather contrary.'

I warmed to her more when she put one of our Led Zeppelin tapes into the cassette player and asked if she could turn it up loud. She sat between Harry and me with the middle seat belt tight around her minute waist. It must have been uncomfortable keeping her knees away from the gear stick, but she never complained.

We arrived early at Chichester where we had arranged to meet Mouse for coffee and cake before we did the clearance. I could hardly contain my excitement at seeing him. His absence from Seacastle had left a hole in my life. We found a car park and walked to The Cornish Bakery on North Street. Mouse had recommended it to Harry as having the best pasties outside Cornwall. As we neared the bakery, Mouse emerged to look around. His face lit up when he saw us and his expression morphed into one of amazement as he spotted Daisy. He blushed like the teenager he was and did some emergency rearranging of his black curls, using his reflection in the bakery's window.

I rushed forward and gave him a hug. He did not return it with any enthusiasm, as Daisy had captured all of his attention. She put her head on one side and wrinkled her nose at him, and I thought he might faint with excitement.

'We brought Daisy with us,' I said, as if he might not recognise her.

'I can see that,' he said. 'Um, shall we go in? I've got a table for us.'

We filed into the café where the intoxicating smell of fresh pasties filled the air with the promise of tasty delicacies. Harry mumbled to himself as he read and reread the menu.

'I can't decide. Daisy, what are you having?'

Daisy bit her lip.

'Do they have one with vegetarian fillings?' she said, gazing at the tablecloth.

'You're a vegetarian?' I said. 'Oh no. I feel terrible. Why didn't you tell us?'

Harry roared with laughter. Mouse tugged his sleeve.

'What's so funny?'

'Your mother forced her to eat a bacon sandwich at the wind shelter.'

'That's not fair,' said Daisy, trying to stifle a giggle. 'She didn't stuff it down my throat. I tried to do that.'

Mouse rolled his eyes at me and snorted. I tried not to join them, but I couldn't help it and guffawed. It took us a good five minutes to stop chortling. A waitress approached the table and stood patiently waiting for our order. When we continued giggling, she sighed and walked away again.

'Honestly,' said Mouse. 'Imagine taking a star to see a manky seagull in a gale. What are you like?'

He gave me a tender smile, which melted my heart.

'Can I choose a pasty from the display case?' said Daisy.

'Of course. I'll come with you,' said Mouse. 'I can describe the flavours as I've tried them all.'

They headed through the tables together and were soon squatting beside the counter. Harry rubbed his hands together.

'Well, I'm having a good old-fashioned classic filling in my first one,' he said. 'And I may eat a second one. The bacon, leek and cheese pasty sounds scrumptious.'

'Haven't you had enough bacon?' I asked, smirking. 'I'm going to go for an almond and cherry croissant with a latte.'

Mouse and Daisy returned, followed by the frazzled waitress who took our order. She scribbled it down with bad grace and stomped off. I wondered if she was having a terrible day or if she was always rude to customers.

'I'm going to borrow Daisy,' said Mouse. 'She wants to visit Bracklesham beach. We will take the bus to the seaside and enjoy a pint at Billy's on the Beach. Then she'll catch a train back to Seacastle.'

I tried to keep my face neutral as I could understand his excitement at squiring the famous and beautiful Daisy Kallis around town, but I must have failed miserably.

'What's wrong,' said Mouse.

'Oh, nothing. I was looking forward to taking Daisy on a clearance, that's all.'

'I'll be in Seacastle a while longer. I can join you another time,' said Daisy. 'An hour or two at the beach will reset my soul after the drama.'

I felt like telling her she wasn't the only one who had been through the mill, but luckily the waitress arrived with our food, and prevented me. The pastries were beyond divine, but I hardly tasted them. Disappointed didn't quite cover it, as Mouse ignored me and spoke to Daisy the whole time we were at the café. I nearly choked on my jealousy, but a glance from Harry made me hold my tongue. I tried to rationalise my feelings, but my heart ached anyway. In the end, I couldn't wait for them to leave, but managed a cheery wave as they left for the bus stop. Harry put his arm around my waist and pulled me towards him.

'Ouch,' he said. 'I could see how that hurt you. I'm sorry. Try to imagine how you'd feel if Brad Pitt had invited you to the beach. Would you have been distracted?'

While I felt it unfair to use my Brad Pitt obsession against me, I had to admit he had a point.

'It's not his fault. He can't imagine how much I miss him. I've only been his mother for a short time. I thought it would be longer before I lost him to a girlfriend.'

Harry laughed.

'I don't think Miss Kallis has any intention of succumbing to the charms of Andrew Carter — as cute as he is. He'll come crawling home with a broken heart and you'll be there to build him back up again.'

'Are you sure?'

'I'm positive. There's something about Miss Sugar and Spice that doesn't ring true to me.'

'I thought you liked her.'

'I thought I did too. She's a little pushy for my taste.'

'Ha! You're jealous she didn't fancy you.'

'Don't be ridiculous.'

He pouted, and I knew I was right.

'We're a couple of delusional, middle-aged saddos,' I said.

'Let's go find some treasure.'

'Now you're talking.'

Chapter 19

The clearance turned out to be fruitful and worth the trip. We found vintage items from the sixties and seventies scattered around the property, including several pairs of Scandinavian candlesticks and some great Habitat storage jars. We also picked up a pair of Danish chairs which shouted designer at me. I couldn't wait to look them up when I got home. Harry chased me around the house, teasing me and being loveable, which banished the blues. Mouse sent me a lovely text apologising for swanning off with Daisy and promising to come home for a weekend before long, which assuaged my hurt feelings somewhat.

'You see?' said Harry, after he read it. 'You're being a silly moo. Mouse still needs his mummy.'

I kissed him and he grabbed me tight, lowering me down onto a battered couch for a cuddle. If my mobile phone hadn't pinged with a text from Brad, we might have stayed there. Brad's text asked me to return to work on Monday. I replied with a thumbs up, not wanting to encourage him to have a longer conversation. We finished the clearance and set out for home in good humour, despite me still feeling sad about Mouse. When Hades sat on my chest purring on my return, I knew he understood. He had become quite clingy since the barriers had come down between us after his lost Christmas. I almost fell over him several times when he parked himself outside the bathroom, waiting for me to emerge after a pee.

I had intended to spend the week sorting out the full boxes from the clearance and restocking the shop, which rang hollow after Christmas shoppers had ravaged its shelves. I also ordered a new fan blower from Argos, as I presumed the offer of oil heaters from Brad had lapsed. Brad's call had made me uncertain of my plans. As Monday approached, a feeling of anticipation rose in my chest as I waited for news from Flo about her sample analyses. George had okayed a rush job in the laboratory as he didn't know how long he could make the Sloane Rangers' crew stay on site without a valid reason.

The Sunday papers had been full of the news of Freya's death, guaranteeing peak viewing figures for the next episode of Sloane Rangers. Harry had bought Sunday copies of all the broadsheets and tabloids, and we had hung out on the sofas all day, eating crisps, drinking wine and reading all the gossip. We had a great time criticising Brad's dress sense in the press conferences. Rather immature, but then we had already established ourselves as a pair of saddos. I hoped Jim had managed to get an article published in the Echo.

The radio talk shows were also all agog at the news of Freya's demise. The commentators ran out of superlatives as they tried to describe the world-shattering impact of her death. I couldn't help feeling she had achieved a fame by dying she could never have hoped for in life. The reaction of the Sloane Rangers' cast and crew to Freya's death did not reach us at the Grotty Hovel. Daisy did not emerge from Gladys's house, and I was relieved I did not have to cope with her woes. I imagined she might feel betrayed by my keeping Freya's death a secret from her, but maybe she didn't care. She didn't seem over fond of Freya, a common trait among the cast.

As Sunday drew to a close, Harry suggested we venture to the Shanty where we bumped into Roz and Ed who were pink cheeked with health after a night and day at sea together. Joy had returned from her trip abroad and helped Ryan behind the bar. I thought she looked rather drawn, but I didn't comment. She often came back from Europe worn out and quiet. I wished they would retire from whatever kept them going back, but since I wasn't supposed to know anything about their activities, I didn't feel able to interfere.

We bought a round of drinks and sat in a snug with Roz and Ed. Harry and Ed had no interest in talking about reality shows and began a long conversation about the merits of the England rugby team. While Harry was distracted, Roz elbowed me and insisted I come to the toilets with her. Since we had arrived at the pub only minutes before, the men rolled their eyes at us.

'Why don't they tell us they want to talk about secrets without us?' said Ed.

'I don't know. I'm deaf as a post anyway,' said Harry. 'I can't hear people talking across the table.'

'No wonder you don't listen to a word I say,' I said.

'Selective deafness,' said Roz. 'Ed has it too.'

I followed Roz to the bathrooms where she performed the pantomime of checking all the stalls before talking to me in a stage whisper.

'You're never going to believe this,' she said. 'I don't know how I've kept it to myself since I found out.'

I tried not to roll my eyes. Roz could be so exaggerated. Each piece of gossip had earth shattering effects if you believed everything she said. I washed my hands in the sink to distract myself.

'I spoke to my cousin in the hospital. You know, the porter.'

I spun around to face her, my hands dripping on my jeans.

'I'm listening.'

'Well, he talked to Deidre Boyle, the nurse who attended to Freya, in intensive care. She claimed Freya spoke to her before she died.'

My heart thundered in my chest with the rush of adrenaline which flooded my blood supply.

'What did she say?'

'I'm not sure it means anything.'

'Tell me.'

'Deidre told him Freya said something about Daisy.'

'Daisy?'

'Freya muttered "Daisy passed" twice, but she couldn't get a sentence out.'

'But what was she trying to say?'

Roz's face took on a smug expression.

'You're the sleuth. You tell me.'

'Freya had been in and out of consciousness for hours. Daisy found her in her room, you know. But what could she have passed her?'

'Honestly, Tanya. I know you like Daisy, but for once you should believe the evidence, like George says.'

'Flo should have the results tomorrow. I'll wait until they call me in to the station and then I'll tell George. I don't want to discuss it over the phone. He hates gossip.'

'But this is evidence.'

'Evidence of what? We can't possibly guess what Freya meant. Perhaps with the results, it will make more sense.'

Roz tutted. The toilet door swung open, and two young women came in giggling. I pulled her arm, and we left them to it. Ed and Harry were still talking about rugby, so we sat at the bar and chatted to Joy while we bought another round. We carried the drinks over to the men who were had finally exhausted the subject and changed the topic to a David Attenborough documentary about plants. Ed launched into a lecture on his new favourite subject, the kelp forest being regenerated off the coast of Seacastle. He explained how much carbon could be captured if we re-grew the lost forests of the sea. I couldn't believe how much his position had changed since the idea was first broached in the town. He, like the other fisherfolk, had seen an increase in the variety and numbers of several species of fish and crustacean since bottom-trawling had been banned over a large area. He had become quite evangelical about it.

Eventually, Roz yawned, and her eyes became heavy.

'We should go home,' said Ed, spotting her torpor. 'We fished throughout the night.'

'I didn't know it was called that,' said Harry.

'You silly man,' said Roz, but she smiled.

We all waved to Joy as we left the pub and walked single file to the car park where two taxis had arrived to take us home. I kissed Ed and gave Roz a hug.

'Tell George about Freya's last words,' she whispered in my ear. 'Daisy pretends to be sweet and innocent, but they're the most dangerous types.'

Chapter 20

The next morning, my mobile phone pinged at me bright and early. Not literally bright as the sky outside still loomed black through the trees. Harry drew his pillow over his head muttering as I reached out and patted the nightstand, knocking the phone onto the floor. Grumbling, I slipped out of bed and picked it up. Flo messaged me to come to the station as soon as I could. I did a couple of silent fist pumps and collected my clothes from the floor of the bedroom. I inspected them and decided they would do for a second day. After I dragged a brush through my hair, I put on my pixie boots. Then I crept downstairs to find Hades yowling outside the kitchen door. I tore open a sachet of his favourite rabbit cat food and squeezed it into his bowl. Then I threw on my hat, coat and scarf before running back upstairs and giving my teeth a rapid brush. Before going back downstairs, I removed the pillow from Harry's head and whispered into his ear.

'The results of the samples from Freya's autopsy are in. I'm going to the police station. See you later, sweetheart.'

He grunted, but then twisted to give me a quick kiss.

'Not if I see you first.'

'Hilarious. Bye.'

I took the car because I wasn't sure where Brad wanted to meet. I soon regretted it when I got caught in the rush hour traffic, which, though short-lived, could be brutal in Seacastle. My stomach rumpled at me and I searched the glove compartment for a toffee or a Mento in desperation. All I found was a piece of chewing gum in a tissue. Definitely not mine. Since I was on police business, I parked with the squad cars at the back of the station. The young copper on gate duty saluted me as I emerged from the Mini and pressed the bell on the back door. Flo buzzed me into her lab. She collected some papers from her desk and we walked together through the office to the interview room.

'She'll be getting a police badge next,' said one clerk to another.

'It's rumoured she already has one,' said the other, tapping the side of his nose with his index finger.

I ignored them. I didn't qualify for a police identification badge, but I deserved one after a decade of putting up with George. The information I had obtained from Roz might break the case too. That weighed in my favour. We entered the interview room to wait for George and Joe. Flo fiddled with her bun and rearranged the clips in her hair. Her bright pink sweater cheered up the dull room and my mood.

'Have you heard from Nick Fletcher?' I asked.

'You really want us to be sisters-in-law? George would have a stroke. The interfamily mingling would flummox him. It's bad enough with Helen.'

I sniggered as George came in. He rolled his eyes.

'If you have to use the car park, the least you could do is act like a police officer instead of a schoolgirl,' he said, throwing himself into a chair which groaned in protest. 'What do the results tell us? It had better be good.'

'It's weird,' said Flo. 'But definitely a step forward, or backwards, I'm not sure.'

'That's as clear as mud,' said Joe. 'Could you elaborate?'

'Well, it's murder all right. Freya Watson died of an insulin overdose,' said Flo.

'Insulin? Was she diabetic?' asked George.

'No. But there's no doubt. It's tricky to spot, but they found insulin in her Ozempic pen. It was confirmed in the samples taken from the injection site on her stomach too,' said Flo.

'Are you sure the pen was hers? What would insulin be doing in an Ozempic dispenser?' said Joe.

'I'm sure. But I have no idea who swapped the semaglutide for insulin.'

'Ah,' said George. 'The sixty-thousand-dollar question. The last person to see Freya alive was Daisy Kallis, so she's a good starting point.'

'Actually, it was me,' I said, making him roll his eyes.

'But where did she get the insulin? And when did she insert it into the syringe?' asked George. 'Natasha Golova kept the Ozempic pens locked in the clinic. At least she said so.'

I shook my head.

'Do you know different?' asked Joe.

'Perhaps. I found the clinic door ajar when I went upstairs for a bandage on my first day with Sloane Rangers. She claimed she only dashed to the toilet, but maybe she wasn't as careful about keeping it locked as she made out.'

'We'd better get her in for questioning,' said George, rubbing his chin. 'You've been seeing a bit of Daisy. Has she made any derogatory comments about Freya which struck you as suspicious?'

'Not exactly. But I got some news from a source yesterday about the day Freya died.'

'A source?' said Joe. 'That's a bit cloak and dagger, isn't it?'

'For heaven's sake, Tan. Spit it out. Who's your source?'

'There's a porter in the hospital who's a cousin of Roz Murray—'

George guffawed.

'I should've known it'd be her.'

'That's not fair. Well, maybe it is, but anyway. This cousin spoke to a nurse who worked on the intensive care ward the night Freya died.'

'Have we got a name?'

'Deidre Boyle. She claims Freya said something before she died.'

'Well, go on then,' said George, drumming his fingers on the table.

'Daisy passed,' I said.

'Passed what? That's not much to go on,' said Joe.

'What do you mean? Freya practically pointed her finger at the murderer,' said George.

'Not necessarily,' said Flo, but George had stood up.

'Get that Daisy Kallis in here too. Somebody is hiding something.'

'You can't believe Daisy killed Freya. She wouldn't say boo to a goose,' I said.

Joe scratched his head.

'One of those Vardy boys told me Freya had been messing around with Zak Kenton. If Daisy found out, maybe it gave her a motive?'

'But Daisy told me she and Zak had broken up, so it didn't matter if he was seeing Freya.'

'Maybe she lied,' said George. 'Let's get her in for a chat.'

I could see what he meant, but I couldn't believe it. But then I remembered Daisy and Freya's fight on my first day at work, and I described it to George.

'Why didn't you tell us earlier?' he said. 'I'd have picked her up on the first evening.'

'I'm sorry. I didn't connect the two things immediately. Freya told me the fight was only for show, for the cameras. It's hard to distinguish truth from fiction in reality shows.'

I had trouble keeping my tone calm. I couldn't win with George. He either called my information hearsay, when I reported it to him straight away, or demanded to know why I hadn't told him before if I didn't. Flo noticed my frustration and motioned me to come with her before I said anything I might regret. I followed her back to the lab where she had a pile of Ozempic boxes stacked up on her table.

'I need to figure out how the insulin ended up inside the pen. I'll take fingerprints from the boxes and examine them for any anomalies. Joe has already set up a database of prints we got from the cast members so we can establish who has touched the boxes and the pens.'

'What about the Vardys? Won't they have identical fingerprints? I know identical twins have the same DNA.'

'It's an oddity, but the fingerprints of identical twins are not the same. I've no idea why that is.'

'If you figure out how or who swapped the semaglutide for the insulin, can you inform me, please? There's something else I haven't told George yet. I think Zak may have physically abused Daisy. I'm not sure it's relevant, or even true, but I need the truth about their relationship. If I ask different questions. I might get lucky.'

'Sure, but be careful. If Zak has abused Daisy, he's capable of hurting any woman, so you might be in danger. Meet in a public place, and tell George if any link to Freya's death becomes obvious.'

'You're right. I don't know him at all. Only what Daisy told me. She might have her own reasons for exaggerating. What a mess.'

'It's horrible. And an insulin overdose is a pretty unpleasant way to die. Whoever did it didn't care how much Freya suffered.'

'They will not get away with it. Not while we are on the case.'

Chapter 21

Brad had moved the filming of Sloane Rangers to the Ocean Café for the morning, but an air of mutiny hung over the cast who refused to read the story boards and sat sulking in the mezzanine. I had tried to park my car near to my shop before walking to the pier, as George would not let me leave it in the police car park. This undertaking took me the best part of an hour, after which I gave up and left it at home instead. By the time I strode into the café, unbeknownst to me, the police had already taken Daisy in for questioning. When I climbed the stairs to the mezzanine, Brad rushed up and grabbed my arm.

'Is it your fault?' he said. 'Did you get Daisy arrested?'

Startled, I tugged my arm out of his grasp and stepped away from him.

'What are you talking about?' I said. 'I don't direct police operations. I expect they will interview most of the cast before this investigation is over. Daisy's not under arrest. She's being questioned. She'll be free to go when they've finished.'

'But why would they question anyone?'

'I don't know. I'm sure they have their reasons. They need to find the cause of Freya's death. They'll probably question you as well.'

'Was she murdered then?' said Brad.

'I don't know. It's possible, but there is no definitive proof. I'm sure the police will make an announcement soon.'

'They took Natasha with them for questioning as well,' said Brad. 'Everybody has freaked out.'

'Will Freya's death be mentioned in this episode?' I asked.

'No, it's easier to pretend she's still in a coma for the duration. We'll start without her next season and dedicate the first episode to her, or something like that.'

I looked around the room. There were several absentees.

'Where is Zak today? And the Vardy brothers?'

'Oh, they're all at the gym for the morning while we film the girls doing a gossip download at the café.'

'I didn't see a gym at the Cavendish.'

'It's down in the basement. It's a little basic. The lockers are the only modern things down there. Most people keep their valuables in them, because the rooms don't contain safes. Let's get going, shall we? Time's a-wasting.'

He clapped his hands together. I wondered if the forensic team had discovered the lockers yet. They were the perfect place to keep things hidden from public view. I sent a quick text to Joe Brennan. He would send forensics downstairs to search them.

I looked around the café. The giggle sisters, Rose and Milly, sat on the velvet seashell couches with Carrie Atherton. Their sulky faces spoke volumes about their moods. They were all caked in thick foundation, and had giraffe-like false eyelashes and bloated lips. Their trademark straight hair appeared to be recently ironed. They resembled clones of each other, reminding me of the Stepford Wives. They turned around when Brad clapped and then ignored him again. Carrie spotted me and beckoned me over to the table.

'Did you hear about Freya?' she said. 'We can't believe it.'

'Do you think we're safe?' said Milly. 'Is there a serial killer on the loose?'

Rose tutted.

'Don't be ridiculous. Freya died of an overdose. The police will use the evidence to discover the truth and everything will return to normal.'

'Freya won't,' said Milly. 'I can't shake off the feeling that somebody got rid of her.'

'And why would they do that?' I asked.

Brad clapped again. This time much louder. And he shouted 'places' at the girls. They all rolled their eyes, but shuffled along the couches and got ready to launch into their scene. I moved behind the cameras where Hugo and Ollie were waiting to walk on the scene later.

'Milly's right, you know,' whispered Ollie.

'About the serial killer?' I asked.

'Of course not. Milly's so exaggerated. About somebody getting rid of Freya, I mean.'

'And how do you know?'

'We were friends. Actually, I think I was Freya's only friend on the series. She told me everything.'

'Did she tell you about her new project?'

His eyes widened.

'How do you know about that?'

'She told me too. Do you think it's possible it has something to do with her death?'

'Everything to do with it, if you ask me, but nobody has.' He made a teapot with his arms. 'Everybody ignores Ollie. That's how it is around here. Only Freya got less attention than me.'

'Well, I'm not ignoring you. It's obvious you are a man with important information.'

He beamed.

'Thanks. At least someone noticed.'

'Well, I'm listening. How are the two connected?'

He rolled his eyes in an exaggerated manner.

'You're not very bright, are you? Freya's obviously been spilling the beans to her publishing agent, and somebody on this show doesn't want their dirty laundry being aired.'

'Why would she tell her agent?'

'Because he's a ghostwriter, and he's hawking it to the publishers.'

'She was writing a book?'

'I thought she told you about it?'

'I must have misheard. I thought she was writing an autobiography.'

'Oh no. Her story would send anyone to sleep. Freya didn't have a life before Sloane Rangers came knocking. None of us did. Well, most of us didn't anyway.'

'What kind of book was it?'

'It was an explosive tell-all, silly. Sloane Rangers, warts and all. Freya knew many things she shouldn't, owing to those great flapping ears of hers and her photographic memory. The public are thirsting for dirt. You should know that. The grimier the better. I—'

'Ollie and Hugo, get ready for your entrance,' said Brad.

'Do you have the name of Freya's agent?' I asked Ollie.

'Peter Dalton. He's based in Soho, off the square. You'll find him easily, if you can use a computer.'

He spun on his heel and headed for the makeup artist who straightened his blond fringe and dabbed some powder on his long pointy nose. Hugo followed him to the girls' table where they entered an orgy of air-kissing, before sitting down and joining the gossip-fest. I took out my mobile phone and made sure it was on silent. I could only imagine the kerfuffle if it should go off during the scene. Brad would have a Texan conniption, and I was made aware everything was bigger in Texas by Kieron. (I had a feeling he was being lewd, but I had not reacted).

I watched in fascination as the girls flirted with Hugo and Ollie, and reacted with hands over their mouths to the latest fake scenarios dreamed up by Brad. They had slipped into their screen personas like snakes into a pond, leaving not a ripple of sadness on the surface for poor Freya, as if she had never existed. I suddenly had a crystal-clear understanding of why both Zak and Daisy had found it hard to separate fact from fiction. The others were also confused by their double lives.

It would be worth chatting to the crew about certain members of the cast. I had a feeling they were more grounded in reality, especially in their cheap hotel. Sometimes it helped an investigation if a group had been treated differently. They were more likely to be resentful and less likely to keep secrets. I decided to ask Finn, the camera operator, a few leading questions on his next break.

I didn't have to wait long. Most of the actors were sandwiched together on the couch in order to fit them into the shot. I had to admire their professional attitude once the cameras started rolling. The scene wrapped after only a couple of extra takes for added angles. I approached Finn while Brad talked to Ollie about some aspect of the storyline. He smiled as I shuffled over to him.

'I didn't think it would take you long,' he said. 'You don't miss much, do you?'

I grinned.

'I bet you don't either. How long have you worked for the show?'

'Long enough to know I should avoid talking to you.'

'Freya is dead. And they're calling it suicide. I can't get my head around the idea. She seemed so upbeat when I spoke to her.'

I thought he would clam up, but he looked as if he might cry.

'You have no idea how special she was. They destroyed her in this show. They knocked away her foundations bit by bit until she couldn't stand it any longer.'

'You think she killed herself?'

'I don't know. But it's not beyond the realm of possibility.'

'Did you know she intended to write a book about this series?'

His expression changed to one of bewilderment.

'A book? She didn't tell me about writing a book, but we didn't have the chance to talk much recently. She had a crush on Zak, you know, but he ignored her. I tried to tell her, but he's the star and...'

He trailed off, and I filled in the blank for myself. Poor Finn. Did Freya have any idea he held a torch for her? I felt as if I would never discover the name of her murderer.

As I left the café, my mobile phone rang. Mouse.

'Hi there. What's up?'

'Daisy called me from the police station.'

My heart sank.

'Did she?'

'They were questioning her about Freya's death. Was Freya murdered?'

'They think so. Flo found insulin in Freya's Ozempic pen.'

'Insulin? Can that kill you?'

'It's highly effective according to Flo.'

'But you don't think Daisy did it, do you? I know her. She's not capable of killing anyone. And where would she get insulin from?'

'We need to let your father do his job, sweetheart.'

'But he's obviously decided already if he called her in for questioning.'

'He's working his way through the entire cast and crew of Sloane Rangers. She's not a prime suspect, but he needs to treat everyone the same. Anyway, if he doesn't question her, she can't be eliminated from his enquiries.'

'I guess so, but I want you to help her.'

'I promise to do my best.'

Chapter 22

Harry didn't take much persuading to make a trip to London with me. He had a van load of stock which didn't qualify as vintage and wouldn't sell at Second Home. He wanted to take it to London to give to his cousin Tommy who owned a warehouse in Bermondsey in the East End of London. Tommy used the warehouse to store cheap furniture, which he sold in bulk to councils and other organisations who needed reasonably priced goods to furnish accommodation for council tenants and refugees. He had long resisted offers to buy the building and convert it into pricey apartments.

Harry and I set out after the rush hour at Seacastle, being in no particular hurry. The council had gritted the roads after a night of freezing fog turned patches of water into lethal black ice. Harry drove with exaggerated caution, but we relaxed as the roads unfroze and took turns choosing the music to listen to in the cabin. The heating system did not work properly, and the cabin became too hot. We both stripped to our innermost garment, pulling over to the roadside so Harry could disrobe without swerving across the carriageway. As he took off his shirt, leaving only his vest, the rose and dagger tattoo on his shoulder stood out in the weak sunlight. I had never asked him about it, because he didn't like to talk about his army days, but his good humour encouraged me. I reached out and stroked it.

'I always forget how spectacular your service tattoo is. Where did you get it done?'

I meant why, but I chickened out. He shrugged off my hand and raised an eyebrow at me.

'Is that the question you meant to ask me?' he said. 'Because it's not the one I expected.'

I pouted at him.

'You know I don't like to pry into your past, but we've been together for ages now. I sort of thought you might tell me without prompting, but it's never happened.'

'What brought this on?'

'Nothing. If you don't want to talk about it, I don't mind.'

'I didn't say that.'

He tucked in his shirt and pulled the van back onto the road. The music blasted out of the tape deck, too loud over our silence. I felt as if we were participants in a dare, competing to not be the first to speak. Normally Harry would have won easily, as I liked to chat and he preferred to listen. This time, the silence stretched out like a piece of elastic waiting for it to snap. Finally, he snorted.

'Wow. I'm impressed. Okay, let's make a deal. I'm not telling you now. It's not the sort of thing I can discuss on a road trip. I'll tell you tonight, but you won't like it.'

'I don't need to, but I would like to understand my future husband.'

'You might not want to marry me after I tell you.'

'Trust me. I'm in your platoon, remember?'

His hands were tight on the wheel, so I dropped the subject and we listened to Fleetwood Mac to calm us down. We drove north to London and headed for the East End. The leafless trees stood stark against the grey skies along the road, looking like hands reaching for the heavens. The frozen fields stood empty of livestock, most inside for the winter. A flock of sheep with a couple of newborn lambs sheltered in the corner of one eating silage from a feeder. I couldn't see it, but I could smell it. I loved the bleak landscape with its frosty soil. It made me grateful for spring and summer to come. I'm a great believer in bad times making you appreciate good times even more. The same goes for the weather.

As we pulled into the compound where Tommy's warehouse lurked, I stole a glance at Harry. A Vesuvian air hung around him, which did not bode well, but Tommy would quench the eruption. I couldn't wait to see Tommy again. He was one of few people who could josh with Harry and escape alive. Most men were too intimidated to tease Harry. Only Harry's brother Nick, Tommy, Mouse, and George had that privilege. If anyone could change Harry's mood, it would be Tommy. Harry reversed the van up to the warehouse doors and Tommy came out of his shed-like office to greet us. He resembled a vagrant emerging from sleeping off a hard night on the tiles. His uniform of a holey jumper and almost transparent pink corduroy trousers was no match for the east wind blowing up the Thames. He had thrown on a vintage waxed jacket to keep warm, but it had almost as many holes as his sweater.

To my relief, Harry's mood lifted like the early morning fog, and soon he and Tommy were laughing and exchanging family banter as they emptied the van. I did not bother to carry anything, knowing that the Fletcher family honour was at stake. I watched them compete to carry more with less effort than the other. When the van stood empty, we went for a full English breakfast in the local café, one of the last originals left in London. The owner brought us chipped mugs full of strong tea while he fried some eggs and made the toast. There is nothing like a full English to gird your loins and restore balance. Harry rubbed his tummy and sighed with happiness.

'Blimey, that's good. I should fill the van more often.'

'Speaking of the van, we should leave it here. There's zero chance of finding parking in central London,' I said. 'We can take the tube at Bermondsey station and change at Waterloo for Tottenham Court Road.'

'Leave it with me,' said Tommy. 'I'll only charge a Lady Godiva an hour.'

'You'll be lucky. You still owe me dosh for the last consignment of furniture,' said Harry.

'I'll get you a souvenir,' I said. 'We shouldn't be long.'

'Why don't you stay overnight?' said Tommy.

'We need to go back tonight,' I said, before Harry could answer.

'We'll text you our plans later,' said Harry.

The tube station sat on a corner near to Tommy's warehouse. We descended into the underground system and almost immediately a train pulled into the station. It took a few minutes to arrive at Waterloo and change onto the Northern Line, and another few to reach Tottenham Court Road. I had not visited the West End for ages and felt nostalgic for my former hunting grounds. The time of year meant fewer tourists clogged up the streets, so I enjoyed ambling down Soho Place at my leisure without bumping into people making TikTok videos of themselves. The Tudor style hut in the square's garden fooled most of them, but it used to be the above ground entrance for a substation of the Charing Cross Electricity Company. It had functioned as a bomb shelter during the Second World War, but now it had been reduced to the status of a garden shed containing the tools needed to keep the square's gardens spic and span.

We found Peter Dalton's building with no problem and pressed the buzzer on the outside door. It swung open, and we laboured up four flights of stairs to the agent's office. Peter waited for us at the door, smirking at our breathless states. He was short and stout, and his pink, sweaty face was topped with a comb-over.

'Hi there. Welcome to the only agent's office in London with free workout included. You must be Tanya Bowe.'

'Thank you. This is my partner, Harry Fletcher.'

'Nice to meet you both. Won't you come into my lair? I'm afraid it's a bit of a tip. I had a visitor last night.'

'You were burgled?'

'I'm afraid so. Luckily, I had most of the older files backed up on the cloud, so it's not a disaster. Freya has a copy of her book on her laptop, so all is not lost.'

He smiled and stood back to let us into his tiny office, made smaller by being in the eaves of the roof and having sloped ceilings. He had obviously attempted to tidy it, but the place had been turned upside down by somebody. Harry wedged himself into a small armchair and I followed suit.

'Can I make you a hot beverage?' said Dalton.

'No thanks. We've just had a full English,' said Harry.

'If it's okay with you, I'd like to ask you some questions about Freya,' I said.

He put his head on one side and narrowed his eyes.

'I'm not selling,' he said. 'I don't care who you represent.'

'We're not buying,' said Harry.

'We're friends of Freya. Well, I am, and we're trying to find out why she died.'

'Freya didn't have friends. She never talked about you.'

'We only met recently, but my ex-husband is the detective in charge of the case and—'

He put his hand in the air.

'Stop right there. What case?'

'Um, the police think Freya may have been murdered.'

He jumped up, the back of his chair hitting the walled with a bang.

'Murdered? But the newspapers said she had killed herself.'

'Was that likely? Did she give you any sign she felt suicidal?' Harry asked.

'Absolutely not. The chance of a book deal had made her euphoric. She was counting the days before she left the programme.'

'Did she make many enemies on the show?'

He laughed.

'Not as such, although she would have had plenty once we published her book.'

'Did she tell damaging stories about anyone in particular?'

He scratched his ear.

'I'm not sure I should be talking to you about this.'

'Is it possible someone killed her to prevent the book being published?'

'There are some damaging revelations in there, but how would they know? They weren't even aware she had written a book.'

'They? You mean the Vardy twins?'

He sighed.

'I was using a generic they, but yes, they, among others, had reason to worry, had they known about the content of the book.'

'Can you tell us why?' said Harry.

Dalton shook his head.

'Absolutely not. There's no way I'm putting myself in the firing line. You'll have to get a warrant. Or at least the police will. But until then, my lips are sealed.'

He made a zipping motion over his lips with his fingers and folded his arms. I went on a different tack.

'You said Freya had a hard copy?'

'A proof copy. Yes, she was reviewing it for timeline mistakes and so on.'

'Could someone have found it?'

'I suppose so, but she told me she had it locked away. Anyway, nobody knew what her plans were. Why would they be looking for it?'

I felt the hairs on my arms prickling under my jumper. The lockers! Had Freya hidden her proof copy in the gym lockers at the Cavendish? How would someone find it if no one was looking? Unless... Ollie knew. I tried to keep my face neutral.

'I'm sorry for your loss,' I said. 'I can see Freya meant a great deal to you. Her legacy is in safe hands.'

'Thank you. Nobody understands. It would have been a best seller.'

'Maybe it still will be,' said Harry.

'No, her parents...'

He trailed off.

I stood up.

'Well, Mr Dalton, thank you for finding time in your busy schedule to see us. We really appreciate it.'

Dalton shook our hands with his wet paw and we went back down the flights of stairs to the exit.

'I nearly laughed when you thanked him for finding time in his busy schedule,' said Harry. 'There were cobwebs on his filing cabinet.'

'Do you fancy a drink or a coffee? The Coach and Horses is nearby on Greek Street.'

'That Coach and Horses?'

'The very same. Formerly hosted by the late-lamented worst barman in England, and a haunt of the journalists who worked on Private Eye.'

'Didn't Jeffrey Bernard practically live there for some years?'

'Yes, someone wrote a play about it. I went to the theatre to see "Jeffrey Bernard is Unwell" starring Peter O'Toole when I worked on "Uncovering the Truth". It counts as one of my most treasured memories of those halcyon days.'

Harry slapped his thigh.

'I don't Adam and Eve it. I went too, with Nick. It was hilarious.'

I squeezed his biceps.

'We were made for each other. It's a three-minute walk from here. Let's go.'

Chapter 23

We headed down Greek Street to the corner of Romilly Street where the Coach and Horses sat unchanged with its red and white, fluted, cast-iron columns interspersed with wooden benches. Metal tables and stools wobbled on the pavement every time someone leaned on them. When I stepped through the doors into the bar, I entered my past. Except for the lack of cigarette smoke, the interior seemed hardly changed after twenty years. The caramel-coloured, light-oak bar with its rounded end. The rows of spirit bottles behind the bar. The mismatched tables and chairs reminding me of the Vintage. Had I stolen the idea from my memory of the Coach and Horses? And the old-fashioned carpet, red with faux Persian motifs on it. A time capsule.

Harry ordered a pint of beer for himself and a half of cider for me. I didn't comment on the fact he would be driving home in a few hours. As long as he drank only one pint, he would stay under the limit. Anyway, I didn't want to irritate him by fussing. I watched him take a good swallow and smack his lips. When he placed the glass onto the mat in front of him, small drops of condensation slipped down the outside and fell onto it. Time stopped. I wanted to ask him about his tattoo, but I went to safer ground.

'Do you think someone murdered Freya because of her book?' I said.

'It depends what they were hiding and whether she found out about it.'

'I think Ollie knows more than he is saying.'

'What about Zak?' said Harry.

'Zak's a conundrum. Daisy had me convinced he abused her, but the man I met was vulnerable and sad. I can't believe he could harm anyone.'

'He's an actor. It's his job to pretend to be somebody else.'

'That's true.'

'What did you make of Peter Dalton?'

'I'm not sure, but he definitely didn't kill her. She was his ticket to fame and fortune.'

He took another swig of his pint. The air felt heavy between us.

'Drink up. I want to visit the Embankment to show you something.'

'Is it related to your tattoo?'

The atmosphere changed instantly, as if Dementors had flown over from Azkaban and sucked the happiness out. I gave an involuntary shudder despite the warm air. He nodded and stood up. I gulped down my drink in case I needed Dutch courage. We left the pub and walked down Romilly Street to Charing Cross Road where we headed south to Trafalgar Square. The sun had emerged, burning off the clouds, leaving a bright blue sky over London. I wished I could enjoy it more, but I had a sense of foreboding. We crossed the Strand and went down Whitehall to the Embankment. We passed the odd memorial to the Women of World War II. It reminded me of Gladys and the other women back at the Veterans' Club in Seacastle. The government delayed fifty years to erect a memorial for the women who served, and yet the bronze uniforms hung empty, as if they were more important than the women who had worn them. A wave of sadness hit me, but I didn't comment.

We arrived at the southern end of the Victoria Embankment Gardens and entered through a metal gate. In front of us, two monoliths of Portland stone were separated by a narrow gap in which a large bronze medallion reposed. Harry led me around the monument. I noticed one side of the medallion had soldiers on it, and the other civilians. The words Iraq and Afghanistan were carved into the stones. It bore powerful witness to the sacrifices of the people who had served and died there. Then, Harry took my hand and walked to a bench nearby where we sat gazing at the monument.

'I fought in both wars, you know,' he said, his head bowed.

'I didn't. Want to tell me about it?'

'Not really, but I should. Operations in Iraq were relatively straightforward, as many of the local population took our side. We suffered a few casualties and were evacuated in good shape. But Iraq couldn't prepare us for what we found in Afghanistan. We survived almost fifteen years of operations there. I took part in the most dangerous ones.'

'What was it like?'

'Hot, like walking off the plane into an oven. From the air, it looked as if a sandstorm had dropped its contents on Kabul, and on closer inspection everything was covered in dust. We stayed in Camp Bastion to acclimatise before we left for Helmand Province. It contained an odd mix of military and civilian facilities. Can you believe it had a Pizza Hut? The Americans and their home comforts.'

'I guess it was relatively safe at Bastion, but Helmand must have been frightening.'

'It was chaotic, mostly. Afghanistan presented a different level of danger to Iraq. You never knew where the next threat was hiding. The Taliban's principal weapons were the IEDs, improvised explosive devices.

They'd put one at every junction, sometimes in the middle of the road, sometimes in a ditch. Each junction had to be barmered.'

'Barmered?'

I didn't want to disturb Harry's flow, but he had lapsed into jargon. He spoke as if he had forgotten my presence by his side.

'We used a detector to pinpoint IEDs and then prodded around them to measure their size. We were face to face with them. We didn't know if they were linked by a command wire and might blow up in our faces, detonated by the same guys who waved from their fields every morning. They would shoot us from their roof tops in the evening too. You never knew which local you were dealing with.'

'Did you work with any of them?'

He swallowed and rubbed his face with his hands.

'One lad from Kabul volunteered to imbed himself with us as an interpreter. He had been brought up by his uncle in Holland, but returned when the war against the Taliban reignited. He wanted to change his country for the better. He spoke fluent English, French, Dutch and German, as well as Pashtun.'

'What was his name?'

'Ahmed. We used to call him Char-med, because he could charm the birds out of the trees. We relied heavily on his ability to get us the local information we needed to operate. He had no fear.'

I felt the goosebumps on my arms again.

'Did he finish the tour?'

Harry shook his head and cleared his throat.

'No.'

'What happened?'

He couldn't look at me. He stared at his leather shoes, worn to look smart for our visit to Peter Dalton, polished to an army shine. I knew it had taken him hours of work to get them like that. I had watched him as he buffed them almost obsessively. He had been uneven tempered since Christmas. Too many evenings staying up late drinking with Nick, reminiscing about the bad old days in the army. He needed to come clean with me.

'I, I killed him.'

I gasped. I couldn't stop myself.

'But why?'

He took a deep breath and blew it out before answering.

'I didn't keep him safe like I should have. He'd be alive if it weren't for me.'

'Tell me.'

'What if you hate me afterwards?'

'You've got to tell me sometime. Maybe you can make peace with yourself today, here, at the memorial. You need to release the guilt you're holding inside if you want to marry me. It's crushing you.'

Harry stood up and walked towards the memorial. I stayed where I was, stamping my feet to stay warm. I knew he needed a minute alone to sort out his head. His tone of voice had frightened me. I had never heard him so defeated. My heart broke for him. After about five minutes, he came back to our bench.

'Okay. I'm ready, but don't look at me.'

'I promise.'

I focused on my now visible breaths as I lowered my head to look downwards. He cleared his throat.

'Ahmed had made plans to return to Holland when we finished our mission. He should have flown out the day before our last recce, but when he heard we had a final sortie, he postponed his leave. I told him to go home, but actually I was relieved we would have him with us. It made such a difference to our operations having a skilled interpreter along. We were sent to rescue three aid workers kidnapped by the Taliban. An informant revealed where they were being held, and we made a plan to get them back. We set out on a pitch-black night with infrared goggles on. We traversed a narrow side street in order to reach the house. The road had been barmered earlier, but we had a man out front re-checking the right-hand side of the lane. Everybody knew they needed to stay on the right. We crept through the dark until the house stood in front of us. I'm not sure how it happened, but Ahmed overbalanced and stuck a foot out to prevent himself from falling over.'

He choked on his words and had to stop speaking. I dreaded the next sentence, but I did not look at him or interrupt his flow.

'He trod on an IED. You can't imagine the terrible luck of that happening to him. A thunderous explosion threw Ahmed's body into the air and us against the adobe walls of the buildings. It blew out a few eardrums too. I had a helmet tight over my ears, so I didn't suffer any damage apart from some shrapnel cuts. When the dust cleared, an enormous hole had opened up in the alleyway. I couldn't see properly, because my goggles were cracked, but I could make out a body at the bottom. I jumped in and felt my way through the darkness, touching Ahmed's curls. He seemed to be unconscious. I started CPR on his chest, but I quickly realised his bottom half had gone. The explosion had cut him in half. I...'

A ragged sob escaped him. It almost tore my heart in two, but somehow, I didn't turn around. I wanted so badly for him to expel the guilt from whatever recess of his mind it had poisoned. He gulped in some air and carried on.

'We had to leave him there, while we rushed the house, but the hostages had disappeared. The informant's tip had been an invitation to an ambush. The aid workers were found murdered the next day. We carried Ahmed to camp on a stretcher, both halves, and the medics tried to make him whole again for sending home. He died because of me. I should've made him go back to Holland earlier. My selfishness killed him. I can't forgive myself. I can't.'

He raised his hands to his face and sobbed. I put my arm around his shoulders and let him weep. Eventually, he turned to me and pulled me to him, crying his heart out. I waited until he finally stopped, exhausted and lifted his head again to look at me.

'Do you hate me?' he said.

'Hate you? How could I hate you? You didn't kill Ahmed, the Taliban did. It was only bad luck that killed him, while good luck kept you and the rest of the patrol alive. You can't keep everyone safe. I know you want to. Being a soldier puts you in these situations. You have to live with the consequences.'

'I'm not the same person I was before I served in Afghanistan, but I'd do it all again. We thought we were making a difference. I still did until the UK and American governments pulled out of the country. I'll never forgive them for abandoning the Afghans. Never.'

'It's unforgiveable, but you can't keep blaming yourself. Ahmed knew. He served his country with his eyes wide open. He died for it. It seems like a waste now, but there's nothing you, or anyone else can do.'

'You don't blame me?'

'Of course not. It could have been you lying there. It's fate. We can't choose when it's our time to die. Someone could push me in front of a tube on our way back to Bermondsey.'

'Don't even say such a thing. You're my entire world right now. I don't know what I'd do without you.'

'And what about Nick, Mouse, and George? And all my friends? Even Herbert likes you.'

'That bloody seagull. He'd peck me to death if he got the chance.'

'You'd better tell him you're SAS. That would keep him from trying.'

He guffawed and wiped his eyes with his sleeve.

'You silly woman. I can't imagine what I see in you. Let's go back to Tommy's place.'

Chapter 24

Harry didn't speak much on the way home. We listened to Joni Mitchell and Joan Armatrading, and let the music soothe our souls a little. I slipped my arm across his shoulder. The tension had reduced, which was a good sign. Following the afternoon's revelation, I couldn't find anything to say without sounding trite, so I kept quiet. My heart grieved for him, though. Such intense grief and blame pain kept inside for so long. No wonder he had been out of sorts since I made him watch a documentary about Helmand. I should have been more sensitive. I had no idea I was essentially torturing him.

We had an early night, and he slept sounder than he had for weeks. I watched over him, fretting, but it seemed the storm had passed. Happy he would not wake up I too fell sound asleep. I dreamed of being aboard a rowing boat on stormy seas. At first, I was frightened, but then I got used to it and it rocked me to sleep. The next morning, we were woken by the doorbell ringing. I looked at my watch. Nine o'clock? How did that happen? I hoped Roz or Ghita would be available to open Second Home. I threw on my dressing gown and tied the cord as I stumbled down the stairs almost tripping over it.

'I'm coming,' I said, pushing Hades out of the way.

'It's me,' said a voice.

Flo. What was she doing here? I opened the door, bleary-eyed.

'Hi there.'

'Oh. Did I wake you? I'm sorry. I thought you'd be up and about by now.'

I shrugged.

'It's a long story. Come in and have some tea. Do you want breakfast? I'm going to boil some eggs.'

'I'd love breakfast. Is Harry around?'

'He's asleep, but not for long. Once he smells the toast, he'll be down in a flash.'

We followed a yowling Hades into the kitchen. Flo dug out a sachet of cat food for him while I took eggs out of the fridge. I sank them into a pan of boiling water. She sat at the small table while I busied myself making a pot of tea and laying it.

'What brings you here so early? Apart from breakfast?'

'I've got some news about the Ozempic pens I thought you'd like to hear.'

'Won't George be cross?'

'George gave me permission to tell you. He had to let Daisy go, even though he's convinced she's the one.'

'Daisy? Really?'

'Well, she found Freya dying on her bed, so apart from the nurses, she was the last person to see Freya alive.'

'Except for me, at the hospital.'

'Don't remind me. Anyway, they had a huge fight on camera too, which Freya claimed was about Zak.'

'What did Daisy say?'

'She said Brad had scripted it to add spice to the trip to Seacastle. She told us she got along fine with Freya outside the show. Anyway, the evidence is not pointing at her anymore.'

'What do you mean?'

'Well, I've been examining the Ozempic pens more closely, and they were not in the correct boxes.'

'How do you know that?'

'Because Freya had been injecting a low dose of Ozempic, but we discovered a high dose pen in the box. They have different colour caps.'

'Do you think someone switched it?'

'Maybe. Although Freya could have done it herself, thinking she'd get thin quicker,' said Flo.

'But someone had replaced the semaglutide with insulin.'

'Yes, but the question is—'

'Did the same person who replaced the semaglutide also swap the pens into different boxes? If not, which happened first?'

'Exactly. Maybe someone tried to kill Daisy, but Freya died instead.'

'How will we know?'

'Ah, that's the tricky bit, but I have more information which might help us figure it out.'

'Damn. The eggs. I need to make toast too.'

I finished making the breakfast and shouted up the stairs to Harry. Then I took the eggs out of the water and joined Flo at the table.

'Where were we? Oh, yes, you told me you had eggstra information about the Ozempic boxes.'

'Hilarious.'

'What's hilarious?' said Harry, giving Flo a big hug and a kiss on the cheek.

'Your girlfriend. Or she thinks she is.'

'I am. Go on. Tell me the rest,' I said.

Harry rolled his eyes.

'Please tell me we are not talking about the sexual prowess of my brother, Nick. I don't think I could swallow that along with my breakfast.'

Flo roared with laughter.

'Don't be ridiculous. We haven't even, um, you know.'

'Too much information. La la la la la,' said Harry, covering his ears.

'Please go on,' I said, munching my toast.

'We analysed the fingerprints left on the Ozempic boxes and we found some anomalous ones.'

'What do you mean?'

'Well, the Vardy twins left fingerprints on Freya's Ozempic box, and also on Daisy's.'

'And they're the pens which were switched?'

'Why would they do that?' said Harry.

'I have no idea,' said Flo.

'But are the Vardys the ones who put insulin in Freya's pen?' I asked.

'Or Daisy's,' said Flo. 'It depends when they were switched.'

'But it makes no sense to swap the contents and then switch the pens. What if someone noticed and switched them back?' I said.

'Exactly,' said Flo. 'But which happened first? And who was the intended victim?'

'This conversation is too confusing for me,' said Harry. 'May I have another slice of toast?'

'I need more toast too,' said Flo. 'This case is doing my head in.'

I put more bread in the toaster, my head full of questions. Why on earth would the Vardys switch the syringes? Were they trying to kill Freya, or was someone else trying to kill Daisy, and got foiled when the Vardys switched the pens?

I turned around.

'If the intended victim was Daisy, doesn't that get her off the hook?'

'It seems so, but who knows?' said Flo.

'I need a nice little chat with the Vardys,' I said. 'What does George say?'

'He says you can sit in on the interview with them if you don't ask questions.'

I poured more tea, and we ate our toast in silence. Then I remembered the lockers.

'Have the forensics team finished their search of the lockers yet?'

'Oh, they haven't started. They all came down with food poisoning after eating a curry. But nobody has had access to the lockers since you texted Joe about them, so hopefully, no one has tampered with the evidence. They're due to search there today, I think. Why?'

'We got some fresh information yesterday from Freya's agent. I think it will be vital to the case. Can you ask him to hold off interviewing the Vardys until the lockers are searched?'

'Call him. He's already at the office.'

'Okay. Thanks, Flo. It seems like we're no further on than we were on day one. It's hard to tell what the truth is with this lot. They're all lying, but I'm not convinced it's anything to do with Freya.'

'Maybe additional evidence will clarify matters,' said Flo. 'Do you have more of that excellent marmalade?'

Chapter 25

After Flo had left, Harry and I got dressed. He whistled as he washed up. It was a relief to see him relaxed again, even if it was temporary. My mobile phone rang in my handbag. I grabbed it, expecting George, and checked the screen. Brad. What did he want?

'Hi Tanya. Did you have a pleasant trip to London?'

'Yes, thanks. We—'

'I wonder if we could film a scene at the shop, upstairs in the Vintage café?'

I had a split second of annoyance at him pretending to care about my trip, which morphed into suppressed excitement as I imagined the publicity for my little shop and café. I hopped from foot to foot with glee as I tried to control my voice.

'I think I can cope with that. When would you like to film?'

'Is this afternoon okay? I wanted to do it this morning, but the Vardy brothers are otherwise engaged.'

Did he realise why they weren't available? I decided not to let on.

'This afternoon would be fine. Will you bring heaters?'

'I'll send Finn over with them. Can you run them as soon as they are installed to heat the café?'

'Sure. I'm busy right now, but I'll call Ghita and get her to let them in. I'll see you there later.'

He hung up without saying goodbye. I rang the police station to be told George and Joe would meet the Vardy twins in separate interview rooms in half an hour. I had my suspicions about how much information they could squeeze out of them without my additional evidence. If I didn't join in, I would regret it. George would call me, apoplectic with rage, after being blocked at every turn. I grabbed my coat and kissed Harry on his bald dome.

'See you later, sweetheart.'

He grunted without looking up from his tablet. I rolled my eyes. Back to normal then. I decided to walk to the Police station. The heavy traffic, combined with the difficulty of finding a parking space, deterred me from driving. I strode along the promenade in the winter sun, which caused the sea ripples to shimmer in the golden light. The high tide brought small waves to the beach, which crashed against the pebble banks, tumbling them ever rounder as they broke their foamy wedges against them. Seagulls whirled overhead ever hopeful of a bonanza bag of chips or discarded sandwich crust. Herbert might have been among them, but I couldn't distinguish him from the others against the bright sky.

I burst into the station, red-cheeked and windswept, after my walk. Sally buzzed me in without comment, and I trotted down the passageway to the interview room. George and one Vardy twin were helping themselves to a coffee from the machine in the corridor. Having often had the misfortune to sample the machine's wares, I chose to wait for something more palatable until I arrived at the Vintage. I noticed the small scar above the twin's eyebrow, which made it possible to identify Hector Vardy, rather than his brother. They were otherwise identical. Seeing each other must have been like using a mirror. They both had short brown hair and green eyes in faces lacking much chin, but with big lips.

I found them unattractive, but thousands of fans thought otherwise. Perhaps it was their fat portfolios rather than their plump stomachs girls fancied.

George looked up and noticed me standing there. He beckoned me into the interview room, leaving Hector standing outside.

'Great! You made it. Did Flo tell you about the fingerprints?'

'Yes. It certainly brings the Vardys into the frame as potential suspects.'

'They weren't using Ozempic, so how come their fingerprints were spread over the boxes in the fridge?'

'They also had a motive for wanting Freya out of the way,' I said.

George frowned.

'I knew you couldn't help interfering.'

'I'm sorry, but your son has a crush on Daisy Kallis and he asked me to help exonerate her.'

'Why aren't I surprised? Tell me.'

'We spoke to Freya's agent in London yesterday, a Peter Dalton.'

'I thought she had a female agent? I've got the name here somewhere. We were going to call her for a chat.'

He flicked ineffectually at a pile of papers on the table.

'It appears she found herself a publishing agent too.'

'Publishing? Was she writing a book?'

'A tell-all history of Sloane Rangers.'

'A keg of dynamite, I'm sure. Were the Vardys mentioned?'

'Dalton told us she had exposed their schemes in it.'

'What schemes?'

'He wouldn't say.'

'I think we need to find out.'

George straightened his pile of paper. At one time, orders had been issued for the police station to become a paperless office, but the orders had been ignored, like most initiatives, after a rash of power cuts, caused by a faulty substation, had cut their source of information off at the knees. Some vital information had been deleted and tempers had been lost. The interview room's door swung open and Hector Vardy strode in as if he owned the place, a slight sneer on his face. He stopped beside my chair to give me a disapproving look.

'What are you doing here?' he asked. 'I didn't expect much from the local plod, but amateur hour is stretching it a little far, isn't it?'

'Ms Bowe works with us as a consultant,' said George, without looking up from his notes. 'If you'd rather she wasn't here, you can ask her to leave.'

'She's not exactly the Spanish Inquisition,' said Aeneas, pulling a chair out from the table.

He crossed his arms and legs, defiance radiating from him. George let a couple of minutes lapse before speaking again. Finally, he leaned forward.

'Freya Watson was murdered,' he said. 'And you are a prime suspect, so I'd drop the attitude if I were you.'

'Now listen here,' said Hector, his voice even posher. 'You have absolutely no proof of that. You've got a damn cheek accusing me of anything. Everyone knows she was unstable. She overdosed. QED.'

He smirked. I could feel steam building up to issue from my ears, but George shuffled his papers again unconcerned. He picked a random sheet and perused it. Then he pretended to drop it on the floor, scrabbling around under the table to retrieve it. Hector unfolded his limbs and stood up.

'Well, if that's all, I'll be leaving. I've got an important scene to film.'

'Sit down,' said George, his tone icy.

Hector hesitated.

'I told you to sit down. I'm not finished with you yet.'

Hector lowered himself back onto his chair and glanced at me for reassurance. It was my turn to smirk.

'Freya Watson died from an overdose of insulin, administered from her Ozempic pen. Do you know how it got there?'

The blood drained from Hector's face.

'One minute, sergeant, you can't possibly think—'

'It's Detective Inspector George Carter to you, sonny.'

I almost guffawed. I hadn't ever seen George so cold-blooded in an interview before. He had never been keen on 'posh blokes', but he didn't meet many in Seacastle. Most of the crime he dealt with was blue-collar, like burglary and assault, rather than white-collar. I knew Hector's attitude would get right up George's nose, but I hadn't expected Hector to be so stupid. George held all the cards in his interview room. He had his faults, but he pursued criminals of all types until he got his man, or woman. He took failure to heart, counting any unsolved cases as a stain on his record. Hector Vardy had bitten off way more than he could chew by insulting DI Carter. I watched him shrink under George's searching gaze.

'Right. Now I've got your attention. Can you confirm whether you or your brother Aeneas have been injecting Ozempic to lose weight?'

'What kind of question is that? Do I look like I need to lose weight? Myself and my brother have practically zero body fat.'

I bit my lip. Perhaps they used the same magic mirror as well?

'Have you ever visited the clinic on the top floor of the Cavendish Hotel?'

'We're as fit as fiddles. We don't take pills.'

'Never?'

'Never.'

'Perhaps you'd like to explain to me what your, and your brother's, fingerprints are doing on Freya's and Daisy's Ozempic boxes?'

I thought Hector might faint. He turned an interesting shade of grey and his mouth fell open.

'Fingerprints? Oh.'

George watched him like a hawk hovering over a rodent as he searched for a hole to hide in. Finally, Hector dropped his head into his hands.

'It was my idea. Don't blame my brother.'

'Why did you kill her?'

'Oh, no. We didn't want to harm her permanently, only make her ill. She'd been threatening us.'

'Where did you get the insulin?'

'The insulin? What insulin? Listen, I admit it. We were going to switch the pens, but we chickened out. Daisy had been injecting Ozempic for much longer than Freya, so she tolerated a higher dose. We wanted to make Freya ill, but not kill her, I swear.'

'Why did you want to harm Freya?'

'Not harm her, harass her a little. We thought we could persuade her not to mention our scams, as she called them. We have engaged in perfectly legal share manipulation in the past, but she intended to expose it.'

'You knew about the book?'

'Yes, Ollie tried to blackmail us with it, the little turd. But it turned out he hadn't even read it.'

'Did you steal Freya's proof copy?'

Hector shifted in his seat.

'No, but we tried. We were convinced she kept it in her locker in the basement. When Ollie told us about the contents, we tried to break into her locker, but we couldn't find the correct combination.'

'Is the book still there?'

Hector shrugged.

'I guess so, but you must believe me. We had nothing to do with Freya's death. I mean, we had no idea about any of this.' Hector's voice broke, and he shook his head. 'Whatever has happened, it's all my fault. My brother always goes along with my plans. He's not to blame for this.'

George took some notes, letting the rasping sound of Hector trying not to cry echo through the room. I scribbled in my notebook, finding it hard not to enjoy my ex-husbands mastery of the interview room. Finally, George raised his head from his papers.

'I thought I clarified the matter. Freya died from an overdose of insulin. If you didn't tamper with the Ozempic pen, you're not to blame for anything apart from stupidity.'

A loud knock on the door made us jump. Joe Brennan popped his head around the door.

'Excuse me, boss. It's important.'

George nodded, and Joe leaned over and whispered in his ear. George's eyebrows flew upwards and his eyes widened.

'Okay, thank you. We can debrief shortly.'

Joe left again. George drummed his fingers on the table. Then he picked up his papers and tapped the stack on the table to align them.

'Right. You can leave for now, but stay in Seacastle. I'll need to speak to you and your brother again, and I can't promise I won't be charging you with malicious interference with a controlled substance. Is there anything else I should know?'

'I don't think so. I'll speak to my brother and ask if he remembers anything else. We'll come clean, I give you my word.' He swallowed. 'And I apologise for my rudeness. I had no right to call you a sergeant. I'm a complete dick sometimes.'

I noticed George didn't disagree. He waved his hand at Hector, dismissing him.

'Go on. Get out before I change my mind and lock you up.'

Chapter 26

After escorting Hector and Aeneas from the station, Joe came back for a debrief. He had interviewed Aeneas in the room next door. It had been essential to interview them simultaneously, so they didn't have the chance to confer.

'I had trouble getting Aeneas to cooperate with my questioning in the beginning,' said Joe. 'You should've seen his face when I mentioned the insulin. I had to put sugar in his tea so he would perk up.'

'Same here,' said George. 'Bearing in mind we don't know what is in Freya's book yet, it seems unlikely they would have murdered her over it. By the way, you need to get a warrant for Peter Dalton's manuscript so we can corroborate our findings.'

Joe made a note on his tablet.

'What made you release Hector so suddenly?' I asked. 'I thought you had him on the rack.'

George beamed.

'I did, and there's no doubt they intended to harass Freya and make her retract what she'd written about them. However, neither of them showed any guilt when insulin came into the conversation. Hector was indignant to say the least.'

'Aeneas flatly denied it too. Anyway, the forensic team turned up some additional evidence in their search of the lockers, which points the investigation in a totally new direction. According to Bill Collins, they found an empty insulin vial in Zak Kenton's locker.'

'Ah, there we have the explanation for the insulin in Daisy's Ozempic pen, as clear as day,' said George

'Zak Kenton? But they had already broken up. Why would he try to kill Daisy?' I said. 'You've lost me.'

'Honestly, Tan. Keep up. This may mean Zak Kenton switched the semaglutide in Daisy's pen for insulin, intending to kill her.'

'But the Vardys left their fingerprints on the boxes, unaware of the pen's fatal contents,' said Joe.

'Meaning Daisy Kallis was the intended target, and Freya Watson died by mistake,' said George. 'But who switched the syringes?'

'Zak Kenton can't be the murderer.' I said. 'I don't believe it. What motive did he have to kill Daisy?'

'We can't be certain of anything right now,' said George. 'But it's strong circumstantial evidence. Flo should check the vial for fingerprints.'

'Did they find Freya's proof copy of her tell-all book?' I asked. 'Peter Dalton told me she took it away with her to Seacastle.'

Joe looked at his tablet, swiping through the pages of the report from the forensic team.

'Freya's locker was empty.'

'Empty?' said George. 'Are you sure they searched the correct one?'

'That's what it says here,' said Joe. 'I can check with Bill if you like.'

'Which locks do they have on them?' I asked. 'Could someone have cut off her padlock to open her locker and remove her things?'

'They're combination locks,' said Joe. 'You put in your own numbers and they stay the same until you hand the locker back to the hotel. They reset the locks to zero until the next client picks a combination of numbers.'

'How did the forensics team open them, then?' said George.

'The girl at reception had a master code in case anyone put their belongings into a locker and forgot the combination of numbers they had chosen,' said Joe. 'She opened up the lockers for the forensic team after keeping them locked since the murder. Once the hotel blocks the lockers, nobody can open them.'

'But what happened to Freya's belongings?' I asked.

'I don't know, but I'm going to find out,' said George. 'Can you monitor the rest of the cast while we gather evidence on Zak? We'll need to check the insulin vial, and the inside of Zak's locker, for fingerprints before we leap to any conclusions.'

'He's filming a scene in the Vintage this afternoon.'

'Excellent. Let me know if you spot anything.'

He dismissed me with a flick of his hand. I knew better than to complain about his attitude. After all, he had allowed me to join the interviews, a rare privilege. I grabbed my coat from the stand in the corridor and headed for the front reception. Sally buzzed the door open for me and I set off down the street my head full of questions. Could Zak really have tried to kill Daisy? What was his motive? Just because he had been abusive didn't mean he wanted her dead. Poor Freya had come off the worst. A girl with no luck. Where was her book, though? Maybe she didn't keep it in her locker? Or perhaps someone else had taken it? Someone who knew the combination she used to secure the locker. Ollie's innocent face swam before my eyes as I fought the wind along the high street to the shop.

I pushed my way through the door as the bell clanged over my head, expecting to enter the usual icebox. Instead, I walked into a warm and cosy atmosphere which felt as if I had wrapped myself in a duvet. Roz came to meet me, her cheeks pink with heat.

'Oh, isn't it wonderful?' she said. 'I can't believe how much difference it makes to have the heaters on.'

'It's fantastic. Has anyone arrived to film yet?'

'Only Finn and Ollie. They brought the heaters. Finn left again to collect some camera gear, but Ollie's upstairs having a coffee. What happened at the station?'

'Can I tell you later? I should speak to Ollie before the others arrive.'

Roz pouted and sighed her agreement. I hung my coat on the stand beside the stairs and went up to find Ollie. He sat at the window table, watching the gulls flying by, oblivious to my presence. I made myself a latte and wandered over to join him. His head whipped around at the sound of the spoon clinking against my cup. His expression could not have been less welcoming, but I pretended not to notice.

'Ollie, how nice to see you.'

He sniffed.

'Hard to believe after you blabbed to the police about me.'

'I don't know what you mean?'

'Peter Dalton called me. He berated me for telling them about Freya's book.'

'I'm sorry. I didn't intend for that to happen. Some important information has emerged from the forensic reports and the police needed to know about the book in case it became relevant.'

'Can you tell me about the investigation? I'm desperate to know why Freya died.'

'I share limited information with you, but you'll have to swear not to spread any of it.'

'Who would I tell? They all hate me. Freya was my only friend.'

'Okay. I visited Peter in London and he told me about the Vardys being mentioned in the book. The police found their fingerprints on the Ozempic boxes.'

'Are they under arrest?'

'Not yet. Look, it's possible Freya wasn't the target of the murderer. You'll have to trust me on this until I can tell you more.'

'You mean she died by mistake? I didn't think I could feel worse, but now I'm not sure.'

'Did you read the book?'

'Of course not. Freya kept it locked away.'

Hector was telling the truth.

'Did you try to blackmail the Vardys?'

He reddened.

'Sort of, not really. Freya told me she had written all about their schemes in the book, but since I hadn't read it, I couldn't carry out my threats. I'm sorry, but they deserved it. They're loathsome.'

'They're not keen on you either. Look, I need you to help me find the person responsible for the murder. Someone may have been determined to get hold of Freya's book. Do you know where Freya kept her copy?'

'Why should I tell you?'

'The police need motives. The results gleaned from the forensic testing don't point to anyone specific. They must be combined with additional evidence to find the killer. Freya heard things she shouldn't and wrote about them in her book. Someone may have found out.'

'But how?'

'Could anyone have got their hands on Freya's book?'

'I don't think so. She kept it in her locker. No-one had the combination except her.'

'Someone did.'

'How do you know?'

'The book is missing.'

Ollie's eyes opened wide.

'Missing. How?'

'I don't know yet. The police need to run the fingerprints. Please don't tell anyone what I told you. We need more facts before anybody speculates.'

'Okay, but on one condition. You must keep me posted, and in return I'll let you know anything I hear which might be useful. Deal?'

'Deal.'

But I had no intention of telling Ollie anything until I stood on firmer ground. As far as I was concerned, everyone, including him, was still a suspect.

Chapter 27

Not long after my chat with Ollie, the film crew arrived to set up the lighting and cameras. Soon, a morass of tangled leads and wires made entry to the café difficult. The floor area of the Vintage did not offer a large choice of camera angles, but Finn chose the window table because it had the best natural light for filming.

'It'll be the only natural thing about this scene,' he said, grimacing as he hauled a camera into position. 'It's one hundred per cent scripted for a change.'

'What's it about?' I asked.

'You'll have to ask Brad,' he said. 'I don't want any trouble.'

To my untrained eye, all the scenes looked scripted. My interest in the process of filming had been replaced with a determination to root out the genuine characters beneath the reality show's veneer. The discovery of the insulin vial in Zak's locker had shocked me despite Daisy's warnings about him. Had I let the handsome and charming exterior fool me into ignoring the real Zak lurking underneath? We all judge a book by its cover to some extent, and I gave him the benefit of the doubt for no reason other than his charming character. I wanted to question him before he found out about the insulin vial the forensic team had found in their search of his locker. George would bring him in for questioning shortly and Zak might be loath to speak to me afterwards. Everyone knew I worked with the police now, so it would be harder to ask innocent questions without meeting a brick wall of silence.

I went downstairs and waited for the rest of the cast to arrive. I pretended to be absorbed in my accounts, but Zak stopped at the counter to gaze at a penknife coated in mother-of-pearl which sat in the display cabinet.

'Can you take it out for me, please? I'd like to examine it up close.'

'Of course. Are you interested in vintage furniture?'

'Mostly antiques. I've got a fantastic collection at home. It took me years to locate some pieces.'

I wondered which home he was referring to. I didn't want to betray Daisy, so I didn't tell him about the clearance.

'It's addictive, isn't it?' I said. 'My house is chock-a-block with furniture destined for the shop, but which took a detour.'

He laughed. I took my chance.

'Do you fancy a coffee? I don't think they're ready for you upstairs yet. They have a machine across the road in Surfusion if you like.'

'What about your customers?'

'I'm afraid we don't have many at this time of year.'

'Ah, sorry I asked.'

'No problem. Christmas sales more than compensate for slow Januaries.'

I placed the penknife back in the cabinet, disappointed he hadn't bought it. We walked across the road, and Rohan, who spotted me, opened the restaurant's door.

'Hi Rohan. Any chance of a coffee? They will film upstairs shortly and I can't get to the machine.'

'Sure. What'll you have?'

'A cappuccino, please,' said Zak.

'I'll have a latte.'

Zak hadn't entered Surfusion before, so while we waited for the coffee, he gazed at the taxidermy fish and the tabletops.

'It's fabulous here. Is the food any good?'

'Unbelievable. I highly recommend it.'

Rohan brought the coffees over to us, his brow wrinkled with thought.

'You're Zak Kenton, aren't you? I'm terribly sorry about Freya. A tragedy to lose someone so young.'

'Thank you,' said Zak. 'She is missed.'

Rohan hovered nearby as if he might join us. I shook my head at him when Zak looked away. He got the hint and disappeared into the kitchen, leaving the door swinging aggressively behind him. He loved gossip almost as much as Roz. I sipped my coffee with both hands around my mug and luxuriated in the aroma and warmth. Zak put his head to one side, as if considering his next move. Finally, he put down his mug and looked into my eyes. I found it more than slightly alluring and had to remind myself Zak Kenton could wrap women around his little finger.

'What can you tell me about the investigation?' he said. 'Aeneas told me you witnessed the police's interview with Hector.'

'I'm not at liberty to reveal anything, to be honest. Have they interviewed you yet?'

'No, but it can't be long before they haul me in. It's ironic really.'

'Why's that?'

'I've been thinking of leaving the show because it has become so boring, and now it's turned into a thriller. Brad had ideas for reviving the franchise, but I didn't want to star in a posh version of East Enders. I only stayed for Daisy. She loves the show.'

'Does she? I got the impression she had had enough of the whole reality thing.'

'That's what she told you?' He rolled his eyes. 'Daisy Kallis is the arch manipulator. She'll tell you anything to get you on her side. The webs she weaves are so tangled I'm not sure even she knows what she wants.'

'Why have you been dating her for years?'

'I'm not immune to her charms. She is a two-edged sword. One of those edges is wonderful enough to make me put up with the other, but I've run out of patience. I'm trying to break up with her, but it's not a simple process.'

'I heard you'd started seeing Freya.'

Zak guffawed.

'Who told you that? Daisy? As if. That's another of Brad's storylines for the show, to mix things up a bit, as he says. Freya Watson was not my type.'

'Why was Daisy jealous then?'

'I don't think you've understood much about the dynamics on the show. Sloane Rangers is indistinguishable from reality for most of us. We can't remember what's real and what's scripted. It's like the fourth dimension.'

'Why has Brad run with the storyline about Freya if he knows you don't like her?'

Zak shrugged.

'Now I want to leave, he's trying to make me less popular by limiting my screen time. I'm too expensive, anyway. He thinks fresh blood will reinvigorate the show and he may be right.'

'Are you sure he wants you to leave? My sister says all her friends watch Sloane Rangers to see you.'

'Maybe I'm paranoid. The truth is, I only stayed for Daisy. I know that sounds crazy, but it's true. I loved her despite everything, but now, well.'

He glugged down his coffee, leaving a moustache on his upper lip that made him look like Zac Ephron. He had the same pale blue eyes and dark brown hair. I tried not to stare. No wonder girls fell at his feet. And me, had I been taken in by his good looks? He sounded sincere, but I couldn't escape from the fact of the insulin vial in his locker. Had he tried to kill Daisy? What motive did he have? I was dying to ask him about the insulin, but I couldn't risk him doing a runner if he knew about the vial in his locker. George would call him in soon enough. Flo had to check the vial for fingerprints, and until then, I would pretend nothing was wrong.

Finn knocked on the window of Surfusion and Zak rolled his eyes.

'No rest for the wicked. Let's make television.'

I threw back the rest of my coffee, burning my tongue in my haste to finish it. Then, I made payment signs at Rohan who had emerged from the kitchen at the sound of scraping chairs. He shook his head at me and smiled.

'Nice of you to pay a visit, Mr Kenton. Maybe we'll see you again?'

'Zak, please. And yes, Tanya has convinced me to try your wonderful cooking.'

'It's mostly Kieron's magic touch, but you'd be welcome to come back.'

We crossed the road to find Brad about to come and retrieve us from Surfusion, his face red with fury.

'Time is money, Zak. I can't have the entire crew waiting because you're flirting with Tanya.'

'Actually, we were—'

'Zip it. Let's roll,' said Brad.

Zak rolled his eyes at me and gave me a quirky smile. I felt my heart melt and followed by annoyance I had fallen so easily for his obvious charms. As he went up the stairs to film the scene, Joe Brennan pushed his way into the shop.

'Is Zak Kenton here?' he asked me.

'He's upstairs, but they're about to film a scene.'

'George sent me to take him to the station. I daren't wait.'

'It's taken them hours to set up. Can't you pretend you couldn't find him? This publicity could be so wonderful for my shop.'

'I'm not sure having a murderer arrested at the Vintage is the sort of publicity you're hoping for.'

'I meant the scene. Please, Joe.'

'Okay. I'll give it an hour. Tell Brad to get on with it.'

Chapter 28

I absented myself from Second Home as Zak Kenton was led away for questioning. I simply couldn't look him in the eye after our cosy chat in Surfusion. He had trusted me and I felt as if I betrayed his trust despite not being involved with the police's decision to pick him up. His bemused admission about his love for Daisy, and his denial of any relationship with Freya had convinced me, but I couldn't be sure he wasn't acting.

I watched Joe loading Zak into the squad car from the safety of the restaurant, accompanied by a scandalised Rohan. Zak glanced about him in distress, but I hid behind Rohan so he couldn't spot me. I felt guilty, but I couldn't prevent the police from doing their job.

'I couldn't help overhearing your conversation,' said Rohan, when the squad car pulled away.

I snorted.

'I bet you held a glass against the door.'

'Okay, you've got me, but honestly, that Daisy is a dark horse, isn't she?'

'What do you mean?'

'I saw her through the window of the Vintage Café. She was kissing someone, and it wasn't Zak.'

The hairs on my arms stood to attention for a second, but then I rolled my eyes at him.

'She's filming a scene up there. Maybe you got the wrong end of the stick, as usual.'

'I know what I saw,' he said, scratching his beard. 'Well, it could have been Zak, I suppose. Why have they arrested him?'

'He's not under arrest. They are interviewing everyone. He's one of the last people on their list.'

'He's too handsome. They're the worst sort. I don't trust him.'

'Let's see what the police decide. How much do I owe you for the coffees?'

'Don't be silly. As if I'd let you pay. Kieron would, but he's not here.'

We laughed, and I kissed his cheek.

'See you soon.'

I returned to the shop where the technicians were rolling up the cables and packing the lights back into their flight cases. Daisy was sitting behind the counter, staring at the objects in the cabinet. She raised her head as I came in.

'Mouse is coming home for a couple of days tomorrow,' she said.

I almost contradicted her, but I realised I had been out of the loop about their plans, which obviously didn't include me. I made the choice to be pleasant about it.

'Yes, he told me. That's great. Is he arriving on the train? You can meet him at the station.'

'I might. Do you know why they arrested Zak? He was distraught.'

'They didn't arrest him. He was taken in for questioning, like you, remember?'

'Oh, he'll be relieved to hear that. I thought they'd found something.'

'Like what?'

'I don't know. I'm not a talented detective like you.' She smiled at me. 'Do you fancy getting a takeaway tonight?'

'I think Harry was craving a curry. We can order one and then walk home along the promenade to work up an appetite. I'll text Gladys and get her to come too.'

To my surprise, Gladys said she couldn't come, but we had a jolly evening without her. Harry tried to teach Daisy Cockney Rhyming Slang with mixed results and we all ended up giggling on the sofa. Hades sulked outside and would not enter, even when I tried to tempt him with pieces of chicken.

After Daisy left, I lay in bed with Harry and told him about Zak.

'Do you think he's guilty?' said Harry.

'I'm not convinced by the vial. Someone could have planted it in his locker.'

'What about the combination?'

'Do I know your password on the computer? Doesn't everyone? Someone could have borrowed something from Zak and asked for the code to take it from his locker.'

'Or it could be his date of birth. Most people use passwords that are simple to crack,' said Harry.

'Zak's date of birth is all over the internet. Anyone could have opened his locker.'

'We don't know he used it as his combination, but I see what you mean. Are you excited yet?'

'About what?'

'Mouse is coming home tomorrow. I thought you'd be ordering half of Sainsbury's'

'He's not coming to see me this time. I'll play it by ear.'

Harry stroked my hair.

'Daisy's not interested in him. She's probably trying to make Zak jealous.'

'I don't understand their relationship at all.'

'I don't understand ours, but it works, right?'

'It sure does. Now come closer and let me whisper sweet nothings in your ear.'

Chapter 29

I slept badly, fretting about Mouse and Daisy, but I galvanised myself in the morning to sort out the shop, while Brad waited for Zak to be released from custody. Brad texted me early to inform me that the police had kept Zak in overnight, probably to intimidate him, but we had no news either way. I wondered how Zak coped with being in the cells. George must have had strong suspicions to keep him there. I couldn't see Zak as the killer, but the insulin vial in his locker was powerful proof. I hoped for an explanation, but I couldn't think of one. Why would he kill Freya? Perhaps the answer lurked in the pages of Freya's tell-all. Somebody was hiding it. I needed to brainstorm with the girls to find an answer.

Roz arrived at Second Home shortly after me, carrying supplies of fresh milk and some chocolate croissants for the Vintage. Their sweet, buttery smell leaked out of the paper bag and drew me upstairs despite having eaten toast for breakfast. I kept glancing at my watch, anticipating Mouse's train arriving and Daisy picking him up at the station. He would be so thrilled. I felt terrible resenting his happiness, but I couldn't help wondering what Zak would make of his girlfriend hanging out with my son. Mouse was younger than Zak, but looking like Timothée Chalamet made up for a lot in most girls' eyes.

'Earth to Tanya,' said a voice, and I found Ghita sitting opposite me, staring into my face.

'Sorry. I was miles away.'

'Hanging out in Miseryland or Sulksville?' said Roz. 'Because you have a face like a wet weekend today.'

'Mouse is coming home today, but he's here for Daisy, not me.'

'Oh. That explains it,' said Roz. 'You can't compete with that sort of glamour, you know. Be realistic.'

'I know. It doesn't help my mood much, though.'

I sighed and took a large bite of croissant. The chocolate melting on my tongue made me sigh again, but with pleasure.

'Oh my goodness, these are delicious! Somebody remove the bag before I need to move my trouser button.'

'Me too,' said Roz. 'They'll soon need a crane to lift me out of my chair.'

'I've got an idea,' said Ghita. 'Why don't I organise a class for the Fat Fighters Club?'

'Brilliant plan,' said Roz. 'We haven't had one for ages. We can buy a drink in the Shanty afterwards and enjoy a natter.'

'Get caught up on the gossip you mean,' I said.

'Obviously. Are you in?' asked Ghita.

It took minimal persuasion. The Fat Fighters' Club had become an institution in Seacastle since Ghita had first founded it. A bunch of us women attended the class to combat excess cake and croissants with box fit and step classes. George used to call us the fat fighters, which he thought was funny, but I adored them. The entire gang would traipse to the Town Hall and spend over an hour sweating to the music and giggling.

'Of course.'

'I'll ring Joy. Can you ask Gladys if she'll come?' said Roz.

'Is it okay if we don't ask any of the Sloane Rangers?' I said.

'You're the one with a galaxy of stars at your fingertips. I saw you shmoozing with Zak in Surfusion,' said Ghita. 'If you don't want them to come, don't invite them.'

Because of the time of year, Ghita had no problem booking the hall or getting our usual gang together for the class.

'January should be the month of the dead, not November,' she said. 'It's definitely the wrong month to deprive ourselves of drink or cake. We need as many treats as possible to get ourselves through the dark, freezing days of winter.'

I arrived at the hall after closing up the shop, resisting the temptation to tell Mouse where I was, in case he sent Daisy along. I couldn't think of anyone I would rather see less. Gladys brought her two friends from Keat's Road, my neighbour, Irene Handley, and Betty Staples from across the street. They were all over seventy, but still spritely as spring lambs. Joy Wells, Flo Barrington, Roz, Ghita, my sister Helen and I were joined by Grace Wong, back from visiting family in the Far East, and a couple of other women who worked at the council with Ghita. We all busied ourselves setting out the steps and doing enthusiastic stretching before Ghita plugged in her boom box.

'Are you from the eighties?' asked one young woman from the council, sniggering.

'No, but we'll send you back to the future if you insult us,' said Ghita.

Soon the Pointer Sisters were blaring out in the chilly hall and joints were creaking as we warmed up with some simple movements. Gladys and her friends had opted to do the class without steps, but they didn't lack enthusiasm. All my troubles melted away as I enjoyed the feeling of pushing myself to the music. Ghita had a way of drawing us in and making everyone feel like an athlete, no matter our level. Her short stature did not prevent her from being a giant in other ways.

As I admired Ghita bouncing to the music, I almost fell off my step, my mind preoccupied with finding her a proper boyfriend and weaning her off her relationship with Rohan and Kieron, cute as it was. Even Flo had capitulated when Nick Fletcher had appeared on her radar. I had to find the right man for Ghita, somehow. She had been an unwilling singleton for too long, mostly caused by her love for pretty men with nasty insides, but I knew her Mr Right lurked out there somewhere.

The class finished with most of us hardly able to rise from the floor where we had done our cool down. Flo offered to give me, Ghita and Roz a lift to the Shanty. Grace took Joy and the three ladies from Keat's street on a circuitous route, dropping Irene and Betty at home, before driving to the Shanty's car park. After navigating the treacherous path to the pub and dipping underneath the unforgiving lintel over the entrance, we crowded around our favourite table in the back of the pub. Joy brought us a tray of drinks and joined us for a chat. I waved at Ryan who perched high above the bar in his modified wheelchair, organising the bottles of spirits.

'I hear you've become too important to speak to us while I've been away,' said Grace, raising an eyebrow.

'She's swanning around with the rich and famous,' said Roz, tilting her nose up with her index finger.

'Don't be ridiculous. It's a reality show. Hardly posh.'

'What about the Vardy brothers?' said Helen. 'They went to Eton.'

'That's why they're too posh to speak to me,' I said. 'Unless they're being interviewed at the police station.'

'What happened to that poor girl?' said Grace. 'I saw the article about her death in a newspaper at the airport on my return to the UK. I couldn't believe it.'

'She was murdered,' said Flo.

'Murdered?' said Gladys, almost spilling her drink. 'Since when?'

'Since I got the results of the postmortem back from the lab.'

'Was she poisoned?' said Helen. 'I knew she wouldn't have taken an overdose. She was far too straightlaced to take drugs.'

'I can't tell you that, but she didn't kill herself, that's for sure.'

'Is that why Zak Kenton's locked up?' said Joy.

'Who told you that?' I asked.

Roz coloured. And I drummed my fingers on the table.

'Honestly, Roz. You were supposed to keep the details of the case secret.'

'It's only us,' said Roz. 'Anyway, we can help you and we won't tell anyone else.'

I rolled my eyes at Flo. She snorted.

'We found compelling evidence pointing to Zak Kenton. But there were no fingerprints on the item in question, so we can't hold him longer than forty-eight hours.'

'Why would he kill Freya?' said Ghita. 'It makes little sense.'

'She wrote a tell-all book about the series. Since no-one has read it yet, we don't know who might try to stop publication,' I said.

'But murdering Freya will probably speed up its publication,' said Gladys.

'It's a mystery,' said Roz. 'Have you heard from Mouse yet, Tanya?'

'No. I guess Daisy's charms are keeping him hypnotised.'

'Daisy's charms?' said Gladys, tutting. 'I didn't know she had any.'

'You don't like her?' I said. 'I'm sorry. I would never have suggested she could live with you if I hadn't thought you'd get on together.'

'She's a whiner. She's not my cup of tea at all,' said Gladys, pursing her lips.

'Gosh, that's a pity. I wanted to keep her away from Zak.'

'Whatever for?'

'She had bruises all over her legs. We thought...'

'Bruises? I haven't seen any, and she walks around in those tiny shorts all day despite the cold.'

'But I saw them. Have you still got that photo of Daisy arriving at your house?'

'Yes, it's on my phone.'

'May I see it?'

She handed me her phone, and I noticed everyone watching me open-mouthed as I examined the photograph. I magnified Daisy's legs and checked them for bruising, but I couldn't find any sign of discolouration or marking. I shook my head.

'I know I saw them at Daisy's house when Harry and I did the clearance.'

'Could they've been fake?' said Roz. 'She'd have access to stage make up.'

'Why would she apply fake bruises? She wasn't aware I would work on the show at that stage.'

'Are you sure she didn't know?' said Flo, who had extracted her phone and tapped notes into her files.

'She acted surprised, but, oh, I don't know. Why would she pretend Zak had been abusing her? And what has it to do with Freya's death? Maybe I'm imagining things. The bruises may have faded by the time of the photo.'

'Maybe you should ask Brad?' said Roz. 'About whether he told Daisy you would work on the show?'

'Maybe I should. But meanwhile, can we please change the subject? I need Grace to tell us all about her wonderful holiday.'

Chapter 30

I left the Shanty at closing time following a lovely relaxing evening, after too much to drink and only crisps to eat, full of Seacastle gossip. Joy poured me into a taxi before tottering back to the pub. When I got home, Mouse was waiting for me on the sofa with Harry. I squeaked with excitement and gave him a long hug, almost crushing Hades in the process. Mouse bravely tolerated my display of maternal love before pretending to suffocate.

'You smell of booze,' he said. 'Have you been partying with your other boyfriend again?'

'I heard she was seen with Zak Kenton,' said Harry. 'I suppose I'm flattered.'

'Give over you two. I visited the Shanty for a girls' night out with the Fat Fighters gang.'

'More gin than gym if your breath's telling the tale,' said Mouse.

'Oi, have some respect. I was working.'

'She needed a top up. There was too much blood in her alcohol stream,' said Harry.

'I hate it when that happens,' said Mouse. 'What sort of work?'

'We were brainstorming the case,' I said. 'Well, sort of. Only Flo and I know about the new secret clue.'

'The what now?' said Mouse.

'You didn't tell me about that,' said Harry.

'I couldn't. Daisy came for curry, remember?'

'Why didn't you tell me afterwards? Oh...'

'Too much information,' said Mouse, putting his hands over his ears. 'La la la la la.'

'This is top secret,' I said, putting my index finger on my lips. 'You can't tell anyone. Especially not Miss Kallis.'

'Are you drunk?' said Mouse. 'Because you're being weird.'

'I may have had one or two gins, but I'm not tipsy, just relaxed.'

'Hm. Maybe you should sit down before you fall down,' said Harry.

'Actually, it's an additional clue pointing to Zak Kenton, but I can't tell you about it.'

'He killed her?' said Mouse. 'But why would he do that?'

'Nobody knows. It may be something to do with a book Freya was writing. It's a mishtry.'

'A mishtry? Are you sure you haven't drunk too much?'

'P'raps,' I said, truthfully feeling quite woozy. 'That gin must have been powerful stuff. Will you still be here in the morning, my little mouse?'

'Yes, mum. Go to bed.'

'I'll take her,' said Harry. 'See you for breakfast.'

I'm not sure how I got upstairs, but I fell asleep before my head hit the pillow and woke with a crashing headache to the smell of bacon frying. Harry had left two ibuprofen tablets, which I swallowed gratefully, chased down with a glass of water I found on my bedside table. I lay in bed with my eyes closed, groaning to myself until Harry shouted up the stairs.

'Miss Bowe, can you kindly rise from the dead and partake of breaking the fast with me and your rodent son?'

'Coming.'

I threw on my dressing gown, which made me feel nauseous, and stuck my hair in a bun before creeping downstairs so as not to disturb my throbbing head more than necessary. Mouse grinned at me as I entered the kitchen.

'How the mighty are fallen,' he said. 'I thought only teenage boys had hangovers like that.'

'You'll learn. They get worse and worse as you get older until you think you might actually die the next time.'

'You don't seem to have learned yet,' said Harry. 'How's the head?'

'Terrible, but I took the pills, so I'm hoping for redemption.'

'Tell me about working at Sloane Rangers,' said Mouse. 'Daisy only wanted to know about the investigation. She wouldn't talk about the show. What's everyone like? Are they the same characters we see on the telly?'

'You mean apart from the fact one of them's a murderer?' I asked.

'Apart from that.'

'Well, Zak's handsome and charming,' I said.

'And may be an abuser of women and a murderer,' said Harry.

'Shut up. The Vardys are almost identical to their screen personas. Witty, snobby and vile.'

'What about Ollie?'

'A mixed up kid, as he appears on the screen.'

'He must be missing Freya.'

'He is. I feel sorry for him not knowing what happened to her.'

'Is it something to do with that book you mentioned last night?'

'I don't know. Freya had a copy with her in Seacastle, but it disappeared from her locker. Ollie's the only person on the show Freya told about it, but he swears he doesn't know who stole it.'

'Could he have taken it?' said Harry.

'Why would he bother? Peter Dalton said nothing about Ollie being in the book.'

'Who could have opened the locker?'

'I don't know. Nobody knew Freya well, so it's unlikely they could guess the combination on her lock. The master switch is at the reception desk and no one could access it without permission. The reception is manned twenty-four hours a day, and they take the key for the switches with them if they are away from the counter. I'm sure the police are working on it. Anyway, they seem to think Zak did it. Flo was waiting for confirmation of one more thing, and they intended to charge him.'

Harry made a face at me.

'Something doesn't fit,' he said. 'I'm not sure what, but something's rotten in the State of Denmark.'

'That'll be the blue cheese,' said Mouse.

'I know what you mean,' I said.

'About the cheese?' said Mouse.

'No, about Zak. Look, I know you like Daisy, but I'm not sure she told the truth about Zak hurting her.'

'What about the bruises?'

'I think they might have been fake.'

'Fake?' said Harry. 'How do you figure that?'

'Daisy took a selfie with Gladys on the pavement outside the house. She's wearing miniscule shorts in the picture and there are no bruises on her legs.'

'Maybe they faded?' said Mouse. 'I can't believe you're taking Zak's side in this.'

'I can't either, but Gladys doesn't like Daisy, and neither does Hades.'

'Gladys and Hades? Can you hear yourself? You're excusing a woman-beater because he's handsome and charming. How could you?'

'I didn't say that. I'm concerned Daisy may be lying. I don't know why. It's almost impossible to judge people's motives when they are such talented actors.'

'You're jealous of her, aren't you? She's young and beautiful, and I should have told you I was coming home to see her, but you didn't have to get drunk in revenge.'

'What? I most certainly didn't. I was over-tired and—'

'Don't bother explaining. Daisy is wonderful and I won't listen to your stupid theories. Zak killed Freya, which is bleeding obvious to anyone with any sense. I'm going to London with her today and I'll be late home, if at all.'

Mouse stood up and left the table, stomping up the stairs, making my head throb even worse. I was open-mouthed in shock at his outburst. Harry shook his head at me.

'Leave him. He's obsessed. He won't hear anything bad about her.'

'I know he won't listen to me, but can you at least ask him not to tell her about the book? That might screw up the entire case.'

'I'll tell him. Finish your breakfast.'

Chapter 31

I pulled myself together quickly after my row with Mouse. I felt hurt by his defection to team Daisy, but I had no time to dwell on my reaction. Harry boiled a second kettle and jollied me along until I had showered and dressed and felt ready to face the world. I needed to pick up a bank deposit at the shop before I met Brad at the hotel, so I walked along the promenade to blow the last of the hangover out of my head. The wind farm shimmered in the morning light and I could see the enormous fans whirring in the distance. Their speed spoke of strong winds in the channel, but, on land, the breeze merely made my coat flap and bits of my hair fly out of my bun. I breathed deeply, feeling the relief of my lifting hangover. I wondered if anyone else had suffered from our night on the tiles.

As I neared the shop, I caught sight of Ghita outside hopping from foot to foot and blowing into her hands despite wearing gloves. Her look of relief when she saw me approaching was almost comical.

'Hi there. Did you forget your keys?'

'I think the drink killed my brain cells last night. I left them on the sideboard in my flat and I've been debating whether to go home and get them or hope you were not late. How are you feeling?'

'Not bad. It took painkillers, a fried breakfast, and a walk along the promenade to make me human again. I don't remember drinking that much.'

'You drank more than usual. I think the Sloane Rangers gig is getting to you.'

'Possibly, and I also had a row with Mouse this morning.'

We entered the shop and shut the door. Ghita turned on the oil heaters, which were still at there. I hoped Brad might forget all about them, at least until the last minute. Their time for filming at Seacastle had almost run out. Realising I should probably meet Brad at the hotel, I considered letting Ghita go home to get her keys first, in case she got locked out again. A memory from my conversation with Natasha flitted through my brain like a winter butterfly, but I did not trap it in time.

'What's up?' said Ghita. 'You've got that eureka look on your face. You've had a revelation about the case, haven't you?'

'Not quite, but it might be coming. It's something about keys and getting locked out. It won't make sense yet, but I need to speak to Natasha Golova about the keys to the clinic. Something is nagging at the back of my brain, something I missed.'

I took out my phone and rang Natasha. She didn't answer, so I sent her a text, asking her to meet me at her clinic for a chat. An idea still buzzed around my head like a bee locked in a bathroom driving me mad as I tried to catch it. I handed Ghita my keys.

'Why don't you pick up your set at home, and I'll come back for mine later if I have time? Otherwise, I'll text you and we can meet up. Oh, by the way, Harry might bring some furniture for the shop today. Can you feed him with coffee and cake please?'

'Will do. Good luck with Brad. It will be over soon.'

'I hope so. I'm sick of reality TV.'

I pulled my scarf tighter around my neck and my beanie down to my eyebrows and left the shop again. My heat-tech gloves were working overtime as I marched up the high street. Grace Wong waved at me through the window of the Asian Emporium. She was taking down the Christmas display in her window which had sat incongruously in a high street where Easter had already made itself felt in some shops. Their owners seemed to think Easter was merely an excuse to eat more chocolate. Hang on, hear me out. Christmas means chocolate Santas, Valentines - chocolate hearts, Easter - chocolate rabbits, Mother's Day - more chocolates, and so on. Perhaps the chocolate barons have taken over the world with no one noticing. Could it be a conspiracy? I should cocoa, as Harry would say.

The Cavendish hotel soon loomed ahead of me. I pushed my way through the swing doors to find Natasha waiting for me in the lobby, standing apart from a group, including Brad and the Vardy brothers. She signalled at me to come with her, so I circumvented the action and rose to the top floor with her in the lift. I caught Brad's expression as the lift door closed. Not happy. But I had to keep going until I remembered the missing link. George often returned to the scene of the crime when he felt confused or the facts overwhelmed him. I needed to see Freya's room again.

The lift jerked to a halt. We started down the hall. Natasha headed straight for the clinic, but I grabbed her arm as she went to open the door.

'Can we visit Freya's room first?' I said.

'Will George mind?'

'No. Forensics finished in there days ago.'

We stood outside Freya's room, reluctant to go in. A piece of police tape still hung from the door frame where someone had pinned it with a thumb tack. It swayed in a slight breeze blowing under the door of the room. Natasha pulled the keycard out of her pocket and opened the door. I entered the room and stood at the foot of the double bed. Its tattered pink counterpane had been switched for a new one, but the windows were still decorated with seagull excrement, and the bedside tables still had wonky drawers. Freya's belongings had long been removed, leaving the room sterile and empty, waiting for the next guest. I watched the movie in my mind, trying to see the scene which had greeted Daisy as she let herself into Freya's room. What was I missing?

Then it hit me. I gasped and turned to Natasha.

'We need to talk. Can we use your clinic? I want to check something in there.'

She sighed as if the troubles of the world had all been handed to her, but she let us in with her passkey. I walked to the back of the clinic and opened the fridge. The small glass vials were still stored in the door. I put on a disposable glove and took one of them out. I read the label even though I knew what it would say.

'This is insulin,' I said. 'Why did you tell George they were antibiotics?'

She flushed bright red and wouldn't look me in the eye.

'I panicked,' she mumbled. 'I recognised Freya's symptoms, and I thought I would be arrested.'

'Arrested? For heaven's sake.' I sighed loudly. 'Is there a diabetic on the show?'

'Yes, but he wanted it kept secret. He thought his fans might go off him. He used to inject himself in private.'

'And how did he enter the clinic if he needed a key to get in?'

She turned as white as snow and I grabbed her arm to stop her from falling, swinging her into a chair. She put her head between her knees, hyperventilating with anguish. I waited for her to calm down.

'He had a key card, didn't he?' I asked.

'Yes. He got one from reception. I couldn't be here all the time and he needed insulin at different times of day depending on his blood sugar levels. He has one of those arm monitors, you know.'

'I didn't, but then you haven't told me who he is yet.'

'Zak Kenton.'

I felt my blood run cold.

'Zak had a key to the clinic? Why didn't you tell George?'

'Because I was afraid of getting the blame and being deported. Zak wouldn't hurt a fly. There's no way he killed Freya. His key only opened the clinic, not Freya's room. Anyway, why would he do that? I've never seen or heard anything about them having problems. And there are many feuds on the show. I simply didn't think he would have done it, so I kept quiet.'

I knew how she felt. I had a hard time blaming Zak as well. But the stark truth was he didn't need to enter Freya's room to switch out the semaglutide in her Ozempic pen with insulin, only the clinic. However, that didn't explain how Daisy got into Freya's room without a pass key. Could they have been working together? My mind reeled. I tried again.

'Did Daisy ever have access to your passkey? Did she borrow it for any reason?'

Natasha frowned.

'Not that I can remember. Wait—' She paused, her eyes narrowing. 'She told me once she had forgotten something inside the clinic and needed to grab it quickly. I couldn't accompany her, so I let her take the spare pass key. But she brought it back.'

'Are you sure she gave the same key back to you?' I asked, my heart rate quickening.

Natasha shook her head.

'I didn't think to check. She handed it to me when I was in the middle of something. Why?'

The puzzle pieces dropped into place inside my head. 'Because if Daisy held on to that key, she wouldn't have needed help to enter Freya's room - or your clinic.'

Natasha's eyes widened. 'You think she switched it?'

'Have you still got the one she gave you?'

'It's right here,' said Natasha, reaching behind a panel in the cupboard. 'I kept it out of sight so no one would find it.'

'Don't touch it. Use a sterile glove. There may be useful fingerprints on it.'

She put on a pair of disposable gloves and retrieved the passkey.

'Try it on the door,' I said.

She shut the door, leaving me in the clinic, and I heard her insert the key into the lock. The door did not open. She knocked, and I let her in. I held out a plastic bag from the roll attached to the wall and she dropped it inside.

'QED,' I said.

'What?'

'Nothing. You must tell George what you told me. As soon as you can. And take the false passkey with you. Whatever you do, don't let anyone see you leave. Go straight to the police station using the back stairs and tell Sally Wright on reception that Tanya sent you, and you must see DI Carter immediately. Okay?'

'But will I be arrested?'

'I very much doubt it. It's hardly your fault somebody killed Freya Watson. But your evidence will be vital to catch them. Please trust me. I promise to defend you if George causes a problem.'

She nodded.

'I'll go. But I don't understand. Who is the murderer?'

'We have two prime suspects right now, but I need to check a few facts before I'm certain. Tell George I'll brief him as soon as I can.'

Chapter 32

After Natasha had gone, I sat on the bed at the clinic mulling over the new information I had gleaned from her. One person who hadn't figured in the investigation until now might literally be the key to it all; Cheryl Barker, the queen of the reception desk, and guardian of access to all areas. Did she hold the evidence we were missing?

I lay down for a moment, intending to take a quick nap. My hangover had drained me, but sometimes being tired helped me explore memories which hid from my everyday consciousness. I shut my eyes and concentrated on Cheryl and her blonde bob. I could see her clearly chatting to me after Freya ended up in hospital. Cheryl had not yet been informed of Freya's death. I had forgotten that she asked me about Freya and if she was improving. And suddenly I had a clear vision of her telling me she had something for Freya at reception. I sat bolt upright again, my eyes wide open now. I prayed Brad had gone to film elsewhere and took the lift back to the ground floor.

As the lift door opened, I caught sight of Brad and the Vardys leaving through the front door. I hung back, but they were busy howling with laughter and didn't notice me. Cheryl stood at the reception desk dealing with a couple who were fussing about their room not having a sea view. Since the hotel faced east onto an extremely pretty square and the sea was a stone's throw away, I sympathised with the strained politeness she exhibited to them. Finally, they followed the porter to the lift and disappeared upstairs to the obvious relief of Cheryl who rolled her eyes at me as I approached her.

'Hello, there,' she said. 'I recognise you, don't I? Forgive me I'm not sure if you work with the show or on the show.'

'Yes, I'm Tanya Bowe. I'm helping them with settings for filming.'

'No, that's not it. Your face rings a bell.'

I smiled.

'Maybe you saw me on "Uncovering the Truth" years ago. I used to be a researcher on that show.'

'Of course. I remember like it was yesterday. You are so clever.'

'Thank you. It's nice of you to say so.'

'Well, what can I do for you today, Miss Bowe?'

'Please call me Tanya. Um, we spoke a week ago when Freya Watson was taken to hospital.'

Cheryl's eyes filled with tears.

'That poor girl,' she said. 'What a horrible tragedy! She was my absolute favourite, you know, her and Ollie. They were the only genuine people on the show. I'd have done anything for her.'

'What about Daisy Kallis?'

Her expression changed.

'I don't like her at all. She changes like the wind depending who she's talking to. And the other day...'

Cheryl tailed off and looked embarrassed.

'You can tell me. Daisy isn't a friend of mine, quite the contrary, actually.'

'I'm not sure I should tell you this, but she asked me for a passkey to the top floor and when I refused her, she sulked for days. She couldn't target me, like she did to others, because I wield great power on reception.'

She waved her pen around like a magic wand. I laughed.

'The last time we spoke, you told me you had something for Freya. Can you remember what it was?'

Cheryl stopped waving her pen and her mouth dropped open.

'You must be mistaken,' she said.

'Oh, no, I'm quite sure. You insisted I tell her about it too.'

She licked her lips and put the pen down on the counter.

'Who gave it to you for Freya?' I asked.

'Nobody. You don't understand.'

'I'm trying to. Someone murdered Freya, you know. She didn't die of an overdose.'

'Murdered her? You're lying. You're like the others on the show.'

Her bottom lip quivered as she fought for control.

'I promise I'm telling the truth. I'm working with DI George Carter and DS Joe Brennan. You can call the station and ask if you're not sure. We have evidence someone murdered Freya and we think we know why.'

Cheryl blinked rapidly and swallowed.

'Is it anything to do with the belongings from her locker?'

I had to stop myself from pumping my fist in triumph.

'It might do. Do you know what happened to them?'

She nodded her head.

'She asked me to look after them after she thought somebody had been trying to break into her locker. She told me they were important and not to let anyone touch them.'

'And where are they now?'

'I've got them. Right here actually, in my staff locker downstairs.'

I hardly dared ask her.

'Was there a book amongst her stuff?'

'A book? No, but there's a folder full of papers. I haven't looked at them, I swear. Not my business. I didn't know what to do with them after she died, so I kept them. I thought the police would ask me for them, but nobody did.'

'Can you show me?'

'I'm not supposed to leave my desk.'

'Can you open the locker from here?'

'Yes, there's a master switch.'

She showed me the plastic box stuck to the back of the booth. It had two separate panels with numbered buttons on them and a master switch with a key.

'The lefthand panel is for gym lockers and the righthand one is for staff lockers. If we want to reset a locker, we unlock the panel with the key and press the numbered button.'

I peered into the booth and realised anyone could reset the lockers if Cheryl got distracted by a demanding guest, by reaching down, pressing the locker number and twisting the key. It would have been simple to unlock Zak's locker and plant the insulin vial there before the forensic team searched it. They wouldn't have noticed Zak's locker was already open, because the others were opened too, before they went downstairs to carry out the search.

'Can you please open your locker so I can remove Freya's belongings?'

Cheryl sighed and pressed a button on the staff locker panel.

'It's number sixteen. Go down the backstairs and turn right. You'll see the lockers in the passageway.

Freya's stuff is in a Tesco's bag for life. Please don't dally down there. I could get in trouble.'

'I won't. I'll grab the bag and come right back.'

I walked quickly past the toilets and pushed the fire door leading to the stairs. The stairwell had dim lighting, and my eyes took a while to adjust. I turned right towards the lockers. The door of number sixteen hung open and the Tesco bag sat at the bottom of the locker under a pile of miscellaneous clothes and shoes. I tugged at the bag and freed it, but several shoes fell out onto the floor. I placed the bag on the floor and picked up the shoes to replace them in the locker.

Suddenly someone shoved me hard in the back and I face-planted onto the locker door before falling over a stray shoe as I struggled to right myself. I heard footsteps running away into the darkness, but I did not follow them. Anyone who had killed Freya for the information in Cheryl's locker would not hesitate to do the same to me. I didn't have a death wish. I got up gingerly, feeling my knees creaking in protest and staggered to the staircase, ringing George's number in the station. My call went to his answerphone, and I wondered if he was interviewing Natasha already. I stopped on the bottom stair and listened, but nobody moved in the darkness. A wave of fear hit me and I ran back up the stairs to the corridor. Cheryl saw me emerge and put her hands on her hips.

'Couldn't you find it? It's not rocket science, you know.'

'Somebody pushed me over and grabbed the bag. They ran further into the building, but I didn't follow them as I was afraid of what they might do.'

'Too late now,' she said. 'They must have exited through the cellar door. You'll never catch them.'

'Is there CCTV outside the hotel?' I asked.

'Yes, we use a company for it.'

I smiled.

'Are they called Seacastle Vision?'

'How did you know?'

'Goose, a friend of my son, worked for them. I'll get the police to contact them. Can you please tell your manager to allow the release of the recordings?'

'Okay. Are you all right? You have a cut on your lip.'

'Fine. I've got to go to the police station. Thanks for your help. We can still catch the killer, even without the bag's contents.'

'There's something I haven't told you,' she said. 'I don't know if it's important, but Daisy and Brad are having an affair. I've seen them kissing in the lift. They think I'm stupid or something.'

She pouted.

'I think you're a loyal friend and you did everything you could to keep Freya's belongings safe. Don't worry. DI Carter will catch her killer. He's the best.'

'You would say that. He used to be your husband, didn't he?'

'He's still the best.'

Chapter 33

I left the hotel and headed for the police station, my lip throbbing. I felt rather sorry for myself after being so close to cracking the case and ending up on my bottom in a basement instead. I ran up the steps and entered the welcome warmth of the reception. Sally Wright looked up from her work and shook her head at me.

'You can't see him, I'm afraid. He's interviewing Natasha Golova, and he's only just begun.'

I rolled my eyes in frustration.

'But Joe Brennan has news about the case for you. I'll buzz him.'

I perched on one of the plastic seats in reception and rued my encounter in the basement of the Cavendish Hotel. Joe came through the security door into reception and gave me a once over. He raised an eyebrow at me.

'Been scrapping again?' he said. 'Honestly, we can't leave you on your own for a minute.'

He reached behind the counter and handed me a wet wipe.

'It's not funny,' I said. 'Somebody stole Freya's book from me.'

'Where on earth did you find it?'

'Cheryl the receptionist at the Cavendish Hotel had it in her staff locker. Freya gave it to her for safe keeping.'

'What happened?'

'I went down to collect it and somebody shoved me hard and pulled it from my grasp. I intended to bring it straight here, but they were too fast for me.'

'Did you see who took it?'

'No. I couldn't identify them in the gloom. But they left the hotel through the cellar door. The good thing is there's CCTV covering the exit.'

'I don't suppose you know who manages it.'

'As a matter of fact, I do. Seacastle Vision.'

Joe started tapping into his phone.

'What time did this happen?'

'About half-past eleven.'

'Someone really wanted that book. I'll get straight onto Seacastle Vision and see if they can send us the recording for a twenty-minute window. How's your lip?'

'I know what injecting filler feels like now.'

'It looks like it too.'

Joe shook his head.

'I'll update George when he comes out of the interview with Miss Golova.'

'Will you ask him to call me when you have the CCTV? I can identify the cast and crew better than he does.'

'Okay. See you later,' he said, but then he slapped his forehead. 'Wait!'

'What's up?'

'The insulin vial didn't have any fingerprints on it.'

'You mean the one in Zak's locker? None?'

'None, but you mustn't tell anyone about it.'

'What does that mean?'

'We're not sure, but it's unlikely Zak placed it in his own locker wiped clean of any fingerprints.'

'Ah, so we're back to square one.'

'Not quite, but our evidence of Zak's guilt is circumstantial at best.'

'And he hasn't got a motive that we know of.'

'It's vital we get our hands on that book. The answer lies within; I'm convinced of it. I'll ring Seacastle Vision.'

I left the station and headed back towards the shop. The raw wind in my face stung the cut on my lip. I hoped I didn't look like a boxer. My nose started running, so I dug a tissue out of my bag. My stomach rumbled at me and I checked the time on my watch. One o'clock. No wonder I felt so hungry. A milky coffee would concentrate my mind after Cheryl's revelations about Freya's bag, but I also needed food. Gorgeous smells were emanating from Gregg's bakery up the street from me. I bought a large sausage roll and shoved it into the deepest pocket on my coat to keep it warm.

As I neared the shop, I noticed Harry's van in the side street nearest the shop. Mouse shut the van's back door and turned towards me with a vintage chair in his arms. His face fell when he recognised me, but I pretended not to notice. I wrapped my scarf around my lower face and rushed to help him.

He put the chair down on the pavement and sighed.

'Are you cross with me for taking Daisy's side against you?' he said. 'I wouldn't blame you. I'm a total idiot.'

'I understood. It's hard to fall for a girl like her.'

He bit his lip.

'Are you on your way to the shop?'

'Yes. Can I help you with the chair? It looks heavy.'

'Thanks.'

We staggered down the street and were met by Harry who spotted us through the window of the shop. He took my side of the chair and helped Mouse carry it inside. I followed them in, panting with effort and gave Harry a smoochy kiss before he could see me clearly, which stung my lip, but I didn't complain. He sniffed my hair and gave me a squeeze. Mouse cleared his throat.

'Hello, I'm right here.'

I gave him a hug too.

'Can we have coffee? I'm gasping and I have loads of news. Also, I bought myself a sausage roll in Gregg's. We can share it if you like.'

'One between three? I think not,' said Harry. 'Mouse, can you dash up the High Street and buy two more of them and a couple of steak pies too?'

He handed Mouse a twenty-pound note. Mouse grinned and nipped outside. I watched him trotting towards Gregg's then I turned to inspect the shop. To my surprise, Harry had unloaded several of Zak's pieces from the van. It occurred to me I had forgotten to warn him not to bring them until the Sloane Rangers had left town. My scarf had slipped down from my face. I caught Harry looking at my lip.

'Did someone hit you?' he said, reddening.

'No. No, don't panic. I had a wee adventure at the Cavendish, that's all. I promise to tell you about it as soon as Mouse gets back.'

He gently stroked my cheek.

'Don't tell me not to panic. You're in my platoon. We all need to look out for each other. Why don't we make the coffee and start on the first sausage roll? If I know Mouse, he'll be back in a few minutes.'

We climbed up the stairs and I took the milk from the fridge while Harry made espresso. Then I frothed a jug of milk to pour into our mugs. We had a cuddle while we waited for Mouse, which raised my spirits after my nasty shock. Harry seemed calmer and stronger again, which had the same effect on me. Soon the bell jangled and Mouse came in carrying a bag full of gorgeous-smelling pastry treats, warm from the oven. He sat with us in the window seat and we shared out the sausage rolls and coffee.

'Okay, slugger, what happened at the Cavendish?' said Harry, flakes of pastry cascading down his jumper.

I told them about Cheryl and my encounter in the basement. Harry rolled his eyes at the part where I got shoved in the back.

'At least I didn't follow them into the dark. I'm not stupid,' I said.

'Thank heavens for small mercies,' he said.

'Could it have been Daisy?' said Mouse, avoiding my eyes.

'Daisy? I don't think so. Isn't she in London?' I scratched my head. 'Why aren't you in London with her?'

He sighed.

'Do you promise you won't say I told you so?'

'Cross my heart.'

'Me too,' said Harry, without a jot of sincerity.

'Well, we were supposed to go to London together, but she didn't turn up. I texted her and tried to call her, but she ghosted me. I don't understand it. We didn't have a row or anything, but you're going to kill me now...'

'What did you tell her?'

'It's not my fault. By the time Harry told me I shouldn't discuss the fresh evidence with her, I had already mentioned Freya's book. But that was last night.'

'Last night?'

'Yes, when you came in tipsy, you told us about Freya's book, and I texted it to Daisy. I'm sorry.'

'And now she's not replying?'

'No. She was supposed to meet me at the station, but she didn't turn up.'

'Could it have been her who stole the book from you?' said Harry.

'I don't think so. I got the impression of somebody larger and stronger.'

'Perhaps it was Zak?'

'I suppose it could have been. He's high on the list of suspects after my chat with Natasha Golova. But Joe

Brennan told me there were no fingerprints on an insulin vial found in his locker.'

'Why did he have an insulin vial?' said Mouse.

'He's a diabetic. But it's possible it was planted to implicate him in Freya's murder.'

'And he doesn't have a motive,' said Mouse. 'Unless someone switched the Ozempic pens after he tampered with Daisy's.'

'It doesn't add up. I need to speak to the Vardys again, in case they were holding something back,' I said.

And then the shop's bell rang and in walked Zak Kenton.

Chapter 34

Zak grinned up at us from the shop's counter.

'Hi there. I thought I'd come in and look at your wares. Maybe buy something to add to my collection.'

'Oh, gosh, um. We're about to close,' I said, a wave of panic coming over me.

Mouse tugged my arm and whispered 'no, we're not' in my ear.

'That's a pity. It took me an age to find time to come back,' said Zak, but he didn't leave. I saw him staring at a hatstand which he stroked absent mindedly. 'I've got one identical to this. And a chest like that one over there. It's even got the same stain on the top.' He looked up at me, confusion written all over his face. 'This is my stuff, isn't it? What on earth's going on?'

'I think you'd better join us for a beverage,' said Harry.

Zak stomped upstairs, his expression livid. I waited for him to sit down with some trepidation.

'Do you want a coffee or tea?' said Harry. 'I'm a dab hand with the machine.'

'No thanks. Go on, Tanya. This better be good.'

'If it's okay with you, I'll start at the beginning,' I said.

'I'm listening.'

I cleared my throat.

'Before filming began, before anyone from Sloane Rangers arrived at Seacastle, Harry and I were invited to carry out a house clearance. When we arrived at the house, we were surprised to be met by Daisy. Nobody told us it was your house. We thought it would be a normal contract,' I said.

'We recognised Daisy and asked her why she wanted to clear the house of such wonderful furniture. She told us you had broken up with her and planned to move back to the United States,' said Harry.

'She said what?'

'It's true,' I said. 'She told us to take everything, and that you wouldn't care because you earned so much money. And she told me not to put your furniture in the shop until Sloane Rangers left town, but I forgot to tell Harry.'

'That figures,' said Zak. 'She's pretty sneaky, but I don't understand why she lied to you. I had asked her to leave, not the other way around.'

'She changed the story,' said Harry. 'She as good as told us you hit her.'

'Hit her? I'd never do that. I don't understand any of this. You've got to believe me.'

'Can I ask you a delicate question about the case?' I said.

'Sure, anything.'

'Did the police ask you about an insulin vial in your locker?'

He blanched, but he nodded at me.

'Yes, I told them I didn't know how it got there. Insulin needs to be kept in the fridge.'

'Natasha says you are a diabetic. Why have you kept that a secret?'

'I'm not sure. In the beginning, I had an image to keep up. The American movie star, perfect in every way.

I worried people might be disillusioned with me if they realised I had diabetes.'

'And now?' said Harry.

'Diabetes has come out of the closet. Steve Redgrave, the Olympic rower, started the change of attitude and it's improved from there really. Modern diabetes control is so much easier. I wear a monitor on my arm. It's a whole new world. I fully intended to come clean with my fans, but Daisy wouldn't let me.'

'Has it occurred to you she might have tried to frame you for Freya's murder?' I asked.

'Frame me. How do you work that out?'

'We think she planted an insulin vial in your locker. Did she know the combination?'

'Of course, it's my birth date. But lots of people could guess that.'

'You're not out of the frame yourself yet. Natasha told me you had a pass key to the clinic.'

'And you think I put insulin in Freya's pen? How would I do that?'

'Actually, the police found insulin in Daisy's pen, not Freya's.'

'So why did Freya die? And why would I kill Daisy? This is crazy.'

'That's why you haven't been arrested yet. Nothing adds up.'

'I'm so confused,' said Zak.

'Join the crowd,' said Mouse.

'Look, I know it looks bad right now, what with the vial in my locker and my passkey, but please can you give me the benefit of the doubt for a little while longer?' He swept his arm around at his antiques. 'It took me years to collect these pieces and I really don't want to part with them.'

'Okay, I promise not to sell anything until the case has closed. I need to speak to Brad and the Vardys one last time to clear up some loose ends. Don't leave town.'

'I saw Brad heading for Surfusion,' said Mouse.

'I'm supposed to meet him there,' said Zak. 'He wanted to discuss something with me.'

'Do you mind if I speak to him first? It should only take a couple of minutes.'

'Go ahead. I'll stay here and make sure Mouse and Harry don't sell my furniture.'

I dashed across the street to Surfusion and spotted Brad sitting at the corner table. He beckoned me over.

'Where have you been? I still need a location for the big night out.'

'I'm working on it. I need to ask you some questions about Daisy first.'

'Daisy? Have you had problems with her? I thought you two were bffs.'

'Not exactly. Cheryl, the woman on reception at the Cavendish, seems to think you're having an affair with Daisy. Then I remembered Rohan said he saw you kissing in my shop while I had coffee here with Zak.'

Brad sighed.

'Not much of a secret then. It's true we've been having a fling, but it was her idea. I didn't start it. Actually, I think she intended to pump me for information about the future of the show, but I was only interested in other sorts of pumping.'

He winked at me, and I rolled my eyes at him.

'TMI there, Brad.'

'You asked.'

'How long has this been going on?'

'Since we came to Seacastle.'

'When did you tell her I agreed to work on the show?'

'The same day you and I did that interview, I think. You may not believe this, but I was ecstatic to get you on board for the show. I like a high-class dame.'

'I'm sure that's meant as a compliment,' I said. 'Thanks for being upfront with me. I'll leave you to your lunch. By the way, why are you meeting Zak?'

'That's none of your darn business, but we're not plotting to murder anyone, if that's what's bothering you?'

'It never occurred to me. One more thing. Do you know where I can find the Vardys?'

Chapter 35

Brad's revelation about Daisy rang in my head as I trundled along in the local bus to the Egremont pub on the Brighton Road. She knew Harry and I were coming to do the clearance. She set up the whole 'poor me, look at my bruises' scene for us and let us add two and two together to make five. I felt my blood boiling with fury. Did she do it only to get me on her side when she planned a murder or was Zak lying about breaking up with her? I couldn't tell, but the walls were closing in on the suspects and only two of them remained, neither of whom seemed to have a motive to kill Freya. I almost missed my stop as I churned the facts over and over in my brain.

Hector Vardy looked up from his beer as I entered the Egremont and elbowed Aeneas who slopped his drink on the table, swearing. They gave me a twin, full-beam glare as blinding as LED headlights on a country lane, but I ignored them.

'Fancy meeting you here,' I said. 'Do you mind if I join you?'

'Do we have a choice?' said Hector.

'Not really,' I said, pulling up a stool. 'I won't stay long, I promise, but I need you to answer a couple of questions first.'

'Is this an official interview?' said Aeneas. 'Just because DI Carter plays favourites with you doesn't mean we have to cooperate.'

'I understand you might feel that way, but you may be able to help us solve the murder of Freya Watson, and it's not every day you can do your civic duty, is it?'

'Civic duty?' said Hector, sneering. 'That woman wanted to ruin the careers of everyone on the show to further her own. Why would we give a toss about her? Whoever killed her did us a favour.'

Aeneas took a draught of his beer and wiped his mouth with his hand.

'Hector did not belong to Freya's fan club,' he said. 'We have a business to run and she could have ruined it by publishing her version of events.'

'I imagine her agent will publish anyway. It will sell even better if people think someone on the show murdered her to keep her quiet.'

'But why would we kill her?' said Hector. 'We're not exactly stupid, you know.'

'I appreciate that, but if it wasn't you who switched the Ozempic pens, who did?'

'Search me. Nobody knew about our aborted plan until that pathologist found our fingerprints on the boxes.'

Aeneas coughed.

'Um, that's not strictly true, bro.'

'Yes, it is. Why—'

'No, someone else knew. Don't you remember? Mind you, we were pretty pickled at the time. Rat-arsed, I would say.'

Hector slapped the table, making the beer slop out of both their glasses. A passing barmaid wiped the table dry and rolled her eyes at me without them seeing.

'That's right,' he said. 'I had totally forgotten. Maybe I killed all those brain cells with booze.'

'You forgot what?' I asked, trying not to sound impatient.

'We were in here after we left the clinic, having a bevy or three, and Daisy Kallis came by for a drink.'

'By herself?'

'Yes. She'd had a fight with Zak. He was threatening to break up with her and kick her out of his house.'

'His house? You mean the one in Chichester? I thought it belonged to both of them?'

'Oh no. She lost all her money in a share deal that went bad. She had invested in some Greek shipping company on the advice of a cousin or something,' said Aeneas.

'Not one of our deals I hasten to add,' said Hector, sniggering.

'Anyway, we got talking and drinking and she told us how much she hated Freya. She blamed Freya for Zak splitting up with her, which was complete rubbish. Zak definitely did not fancy Freya. I think there was something else between Daisy and Freya, but she wouldn't admit it,' said Aeneas.

'Then I told her about our plan to switch the boxes to make Freya ill and how we had chickened out at the last moment.'

'Literally. Which is why the boxes had our fingerprints on them.'

'What did she say?'

'She called us cowards,' said Hector. 'And laughed at us.'

'Then she called a taxi and went home without telling us.'

'Did you ever discuss it again?' I said.

'No, never. We left well alone. We've had a good run with the show. If this is the end, we've made shed loads of money,' said Hector.

'All invested in prime real estate,' said Aeneas. 'We'll never have to work again.'

They chinked their glasses together and took a swig of their beers. A wave of loathing washed over me and I stood up to go.

'Leaving so soon?' said Hector.

'Can't be soon enough for me,' I muttered as I started for the door.

Then something hit me.

'How did you get into the clinic in the first place?'

'Oh, we waited for Natasha to go to the toilet. Everyone knew she left the clinic unlocked when she needed a quick tinkle.'

I exited the pub, rigid with indignation. What a pair of prats. My mobile phone pinged in my handbag. I dug it out and screwed my eyes up to see the screen. A message from George asking me to return to the station as soon as I could. I texted Harry and Mouse to let them know where I would be and hurried to the station, my heart in my mouth. The facts were piling up, but in which order would they fall? The case reminded me of a game of Mikado. It was hard to find one clue without changing the significance of another.

I took a bus back to the station and ran up the steps, an action I immediately regretted as my calves were so tight from Ghita's step class. Sally Wright buzzed me through without chatting.

'They're waiting for you in the main interview room,' she said, flicking her hair towards the security door. Intrigued, I strode down the corridor and let myself in. George and Joe were already seated at the table and they were watching a CCTV recording which I realised came from the cellar door of the Cavendish hotel. They replayed it backwards and forwards as I sat down and then paused it on the screen. The face of Ollie

Matthews gazed out at me as he held a Tesco bag under his arm.

'Bingo,' said George. 'We have our murderer.'

'Sorry. What? No, I don't think so,' I said.

'He's the guy who knocked you down in the Cavendish hotel's basement and stole Freya's book,' said Joe. 'What more do you need?'

'Oh, yes. That's highly possible, but he didn't kill anyone. He's more interested in blackmailing members of the show using Freya's research. I expect he would be next to die if we don't arrest the murderer soon.'

'We? You leave the arresting up to us. We still need to speak to this Ollie Matthews.'

'Is he coming in?'

'Yes, uniform have picked him up and they should be here shortly,' said Joe.

'What's your theory, Tan?' asked George.

'It's more of a plan, really. I think we should use the book to set a trap for the killer.'

'How so?'

'Well, Jim Swift at the Worthing Echo owes me a favour. We should ask him to publish an article online tonight about Freya's book and how it went missing, but now is in the proud possession of Ollie Matthews, Freya Watson's faithful friend. I can alert Roz so she spreads the gossip far and wide and makes sure everyone hears about it, especially members of the Sloane Rangers cast and crew. My guess is that someone will come looking for the book.'

'We lie in wait in Ollie's room? But how will they get in?'

'The murderer has a passkey. That's how they entered the clinic and tampered with the syringes. I think I know how it was done, but first we need to arrest the person who enters Ollie's room to confirm my theory.'

'Can't you tell us?'

'I'd rather see who tries to steal the book first. My theory will change depending on their identity. I suspect the book will contain a powerful motive for whoever that is.'

'You never fail to amaze me. I guess with all those years together it's hardly surprising my skills rubbed off on you,' said George, grinning.

'That must be what happened,' I said.

Two uniformed officers delivered Ollie Matthews to the interview room shortly afterwards. We left the recording of him exiting the hotel basement up on the screen and he did not bother to deny its content.

'Are you okay?' he asked me. 'I didn't mean to shove you so hard. I was desperate to lay my hands on the book and I heard you talking to Cheryl at reception.'

'What do you need it for?' I said.

He shrugged.

'Freya told me it contained compromising information about every member of the cast. I thought since one of them had murdered her over it, the least I could do was get revenge by blackmailing them. Nobody treated her kindly except me.'

'We'll ignore the bit about blackmail for now,' said George. 'Do you realise possessing the book puts you in grave danger?'

Ollie snorted.

'What sort of danger?'

'The person who murdered Freya wanted the book. Don't you think they'd happily murder you too?'

'I hadn't thought of that.'

'No, I didn't think you had,' said George. 'We need you to help us trap them, and I'll see if I can get you lenient treatment from the courts.'

'I'd rather be let off with a caution,' said Ollie.

'Listen, you cheeky little—'

'Now, DI Carter, don't let him get to you,' said Joe, trying not to smirk. 'I'm sure Ollie is going to give us his full cooperation.'

'Hm. I suppose so. What do you want me to do?'

Chapter 36

After being caught red-handed with Freya's bag, Ollie Matthews proved to be relatively cooperative, and we soon had a full confession. George laid in the bones of a plan to catch the murderer and we set it up. Jim Swift proved his worth by issuing an article online about Ollie's stewardship of Freya's book almost immediately after George contacted him. He stressed how luck had preserved the sole copies of the book on Freyas laptop and her hard copy, despite the burglary in London. Roz could hardly believe her ears when George asked her to spread the story rather than keep it to herself, her serious gossip habit having irritated him beyond measure in the past. I called Helen and asked her to visit Gladys for tea and a chat to make sure Daisy heard about the book. She did not sound keen at the beginning.

'I thought you were getting me work as an extra on the show,' said Helen.

'You're complaining about being a lead character in real life?' I said. 'Sometimes I don't understand you.'

'All right. I'm game. When do you need me?'

'Can you go straight there?'

'Sure. I'll go now. Does Gladys know about this plan?'

'No, but we can explain later. It will be easier to pull off if one of you isn't acting. Good luck.'

'Thanks.'

'And watch out for Daisy. If she's behind the death of Freya, she's more dangerous than she looks.'

'I'm dating a Detective Inspector; danger is my middle name.'

I couldn't help laughing at her, and she cut off our call in a snot with me. Sisters!

Mouse and Harry were agog at the increased pace of the investigation. Harry wanted me to stay at home while George and Joe did their stuff, but although they were convinced the murderer would be one of two people, they wanted me there to identify anyone else who turned up. Ghita and Roz went to the Grotty Hovel with them, desperate to follow proceedings. They all kept an eye on Gladys's house next door, to warn us of Daisy's movements. From the stifled giggling I heard when I rang to check on them, they weren't taking their duties too seriously.

George and Joe headed for the Cavendish with me in tow. But Ollie himself had been detained in a cell at the station to avoid misunderstandings. Cheryl Barker agreed to call Ollie's room if she saw anyone entering the lift to come upstairs. We let ourselves into Ollie's room, which only contained one armchair and a single bed. Joe and I were forced to perch on the bed while George took the chair. The tension rose as we sat around waiting for the news article to work its magic. Meanwhile, we put on disposable gloves and divided the pages from the folder into three piles of similar thickness.

Any boredom we might have felt on a normal stakeout vanished in minutes as we skim-read the contents. George guffawed several times without explaining what had amused him so much. Joe slapped his thigh and muttered, 'I don't believe it' more than once. The pages I had been allocated were more sedate in their content. I almost dozed off at Freya's account of her early life. Ollie had been right about Sloane Rangers being the start of everything for her. Her upbringing had been staid and boring without a single incident or accident to liven it up. But then Freya's account of Daisy Kallis's early life filled my pages instead, as the page numbers leapt ahead in order. The tale riveted me from the first page, but the hairs on my arms stood up when Daisy applied for, and was accepted, for nurses' training in her native Greece. I tried to imagine her looking after sick patients, but failed. Somebody so self-centred would never have made a wonderful nurse, but it explained where she picked up the expertise to tamper with the Ozempic pens, and the knowledge of insulin to use it as a poison.

'George? I've got something here,' I said. 'Daisy Kallis trained as a nurse.'

'And they dismissed her for malpractice,' said Joe, waving a piece of paper at me. 'We are reading two halves of the same story.'

'Have you found anything sinister in there about Zak?' I asked.

'Nothing. There's some conspiracy theory nonsense about the Vardys, and suggestions Brad may have been brought in to shut down the show, but nothing earth shattering. We need to wait here and confirm Tan's theories,' said George.

Outside the hotel, most of Seacastle had sunk into sleep. Only the odd shriek from drunken couples flirting on their way home broke the silence. Anticipation kept me awake as we finished our sections of the book and handed them around. The editors would have their work cut out to make it into a bestseller despite the content. Freya's prose felt turgid and plodding, like a dull policeman telling you about an arrest for littering. Perhaps Freya's parents would decide to leave sleeping dogs lie once the police charged somebody with the murder of their daughter, and quietly shelve the book without publishing it.

A faint clicking noise echoed through the quiet room as someone slid a keycard into the door lock. My heart rate sped up. George stayed sitting, pretending to read his pages of Freya's book. Joe and I both stood up, and he moved swiftly to stand behind the door. The door opened and Daisy Kallis came in, checking the corridor behind her to make sure wasn't followed. As she turned to examine the room, she spotted George, and she froze long enough for Joe to shut the door behind her, trapping her inside. He grabbed the keycard out of her hand, still wearing a disposable glove.

'You won't be needing this anymore,' he said, inserting it into an evidence bag.

'Ah, Miss Kallis, how kind of you to join us,' said George. 'I expect you were hoping to get your hands on this book proof. I don't know why. It's not exactly Jack Reacher.'

Daisy's mouth opened in protest, but nothing came out at first. Then she turned to me.

'What's going on? I don't understand.'

'We are here to arrest you for the murder of Freya Watson. Anything you say may be used in evidence against you,' said George. 'I think it's pretty obvious.'

'Murder Freya? Why would I do that?'

'You had a pretty powerful motive as far as I can see,' said Joe. 'Her research into your past dug up a few nasty stories. I doubt your fans would approve of you forcing dying patients to name you in their wills. You must have been desperate to destroy the files and any copy of the book before the publisher got hold of them.'

'Kind sweet Daisy Kallis. Your carefully constructed image would fly away the minute they published this book,' I said. 'You certainly had my son fooled. Were you using him to find out about the case?'

She sneered at me.

'You don't think I'd lower myself to fancy a man with no future, do you?'

'Why did you seduce Brad? Were you trying to make Zak jealous? I think you were hoping for an explosive argument to back up your elaborate plot,' said Joe.

'What plot? You're all grasping at straws. Zak tried to murder me. You have the evidence from his locker.'

'What evidence?' said George.

'The insulin bottle. I should have told you Zak is a diabetic. He wanted to get rid of me so he could have Freya.'

'But you're not dead,' I said. 'Freya is. Why would he swap the syringes around?'

'But that was the Vardys,' said Daisy. 'Their fingerprints were on the boxes. Mouse told me.'

'Unfortunately for you, I spoke to the Vardys yesterday, and they admitted to telling you about their failed plan in a pub before Freya died. You switched the pens yourself after loading yours up with insulin, killing two birds with one stone.'

'Freya dead and Zak framed for murder. The perfect revenge,' said George.

'You can't prove any of this.'

'This passkey is pretty solid proof,' said Joe, swinging the bag in front of her nose. 'As well as your powerful motive, you are the only one of the cast who had the medical knowledge to tamper with the syringes, and the only one with a pass key to all areas. What viable excuse can you have for coming to Ollie's room after Helen told you Ollie had Freya's book?'

'And how did you know about the insulin bottle in Zak's locker?' said George. 'That information has not been released to the public.'

'Mouse told me.'

'No, he didn't. He doesn't know about it. I'm the only person outside the station who has that information and I haven't told anyone about it,' I said.

Daisy deflated slightly.

'I would have killed Zak, if I had decided to kill anyone,' she said. 'He wanted to leave me after all I did for him. He threw me out of our house.'

'Was that after he discovered you were sleeping with Brad?' I said. 'The poor man is so loyal he kept making excuses for you until he realised you had given away his precious antiques.'

'He loved them more than me. I should have cut them up and burned them when he abused me.'

'That old chestnut. I saw the photo you took with Gladys. All your bruises had miraculously disappeared after you made sure Harry and I saw them.'

'What happened to Freya's laptop?' said Daisy. 'I don't see it here. Does Ollie have it?'

'And why would you care?' said Joe. 'We're taking you directly to the station.'

'You should destroy it. That book is poison. It will ruin the series and the careers of everyone on it.'

'As if you cared about anyone else,' I said.

'Why have you broken into Ollie's room? Were you planning on killing him to get rid of the evidence?'

'You don't know what you're talking about,' said Daisy, holding her bag behind her back.

'I'm willing to bet your bag contains another syringe,' said George. 'Or had you cooked up a unique plan? Why don't you give it to me?'

Daisy reached into the bag and took out a syringe, pointing it at me.

'You'll have to make me,' she said.

I tensed, unsure if I had the reactions to escape her lunging at me. Suddenly, the door swung open, knocking her to the floor. The syringe flew through the air and landed on the floor beside me. I picked it up with caution. Cheryl Barker sat on Daisy Kallis, holding a laptop with flower stickers on it.

'Sorry I'm late,' she said. 'I couldn't get a call through to this room. I thought you might need this.'

Joe offered her a hand and then lifted a winded Daisy from the carpet. Before she could protest, he recited her rights officially while putting handcuffs on her. George collected the pages of Freya's book into the folder and tucked it under his arm.

'Who the devil are you?' he said.

'Oh, Cheryl, Cheryl Barker. I work on reception. I've brought you Freya's laptop. It got left in my locker when the Tesco bag was taken from Tanya.'

'A pleasure to meet you, Miss Barker. I hope you'll come down to the station tomorrow and give us a statement. I'd like the laptop now though, if that's all right with you.'

'It's all yours,' said Cheryl. 'Dangerous things laptops.'

George put it into Freya's Tesco bag with the folder.

'That's that,' he said. 'Let's get Miss Kallis locked up for the night in a nice, comfy cell.'

Chapter 37

The circus packed up and left town as soon as news spread about Daisy Kallis being charged with murder. George let Ollie off with a caution which I felt may have been over-generous since he showed zero remorse for trying to blackmail the Vardys. I didn't feel inclined to exchange fond farewells with anyone on the cast. They all deserved each other as far as I was concerned. My brush with reality television had convinced me my life in Seacastle scored highly on the idyllic metre despite periods of near penury. I wouldn't swap my band of fat fighters and assorted family for all the tea in China. I also realised my dreams of returning to television were probably more likely to generate nightmares rather than fairy tales. My chances of being paid for my brief foray into show business were vanishingly slim, but I didn't care. The lesson seemed compensation enough.

Mouse had gone back to university suitably chastened. I didn't blame him for his behaviour. Falling for a star in real life would tax the emotions of most young men and stretch the boundaries of their credibility in the case of Daisy Kallis. She had manipulated us all. Well, everyone except George, really. He never fell for her charms. In his dogged way, he stuck to his guns and the evidence and never let the stardust blind him. I had to hand it to him. He still had a lot to teach me about sleuthing, whether I liked it or not.

In a strange way, the entire debacle had worked out perfectly for Harry and me. Zak had visited the shop again after Daisy's arrest, stopping for a coffee and a slice of Ghita's latest creation, another variation on the pomegranate theme. He promptly ordered one to take home with him. He had also asked for details of the investigation, but I told him he would have to wait for the press to get their claws into the story. After finishing his coffee and cake, he had completed a tour of the shop and stroked all his furniture like someone caressing their beloved pets, and asked us if we could deliver them back to the house he had shared with Daisy. Harry inquired if he could pay for the petrol, and Zak had offered us a large sum of money to buy back his furniture instead. We tried to refuse, not that hard if I'm honest, but Zak insisted. He could afford it, so we agreed to what amounted to a fantastic price for us and a modest amount for him.

The journey back to Zak's house had a surreal quality about it. I had a serious case of déjà vu as we turned into the village where it stood. The house had not grown on me with a second visit. Modern houses are not my thing. We sat outside in the van for a moment before ringing the doorbell.

'This is the first time I've been asked to reverse a clearance,' said Harry. 'It feels like Superman made the earth spin backwards again.'

'It's a bizarre experience,' I said. 'Being paid for it makes it even weirder.'

'Poor Zak. Daisy's betrayal has hit him hard. I suppose it's not surprising really. Trust is the only irreplaceable element in a relationship. It's the glue that holds everything else together.'

'Once that fails, the entire edifice comes tumbling down. That's why I wanted to know about your tattoo. The more you hide from me, the harder it is to trust you.'

Harry frowned.

'You don't trust me?'

'Of course I do. But I need you to tell me about the things you are hiding from me. I haven't hidden anything from you.'

'I've told you most things. There are some secrets that aren't mine to tell.'

'Like what.'

Harry laughed.

'Hilarious. I can't tell you. Nick would kill me.'

'Nick? What's he hiding?'

'Maybe you should ask your girl, Flo?'

'As if Flo would tell me any of her secrets. She only tells me George's.'

'The phrase tangled webs springs to mind.'

'I know what you mean.'

The front door opened, and Zak came out, beaming.

'Hi folks,' he said. 'I thought I heard you arriving. Let's get to work.'

Behind him, a slim blonde woman appeared at the door with bare feet. She waved at us and I waved back.

'That's Kim,' said Zak. 'She's staying with me.'

Harry raised an eyebrow at me as Zak headed for the back of the van.

'That didn't take long,' whispered Harry, and I shrugged at him.

Zak had every right to take advantage of his single state. I hoped she would be nicer than Daisy. We carried Zak's precious pieces back inside the house, one by one and watched as he carefully manoeuvred them into their designated spots, crooning with appreciation. I could imagine Daisy's annoyance at his obsession. She had to be the centre of attention all the time to keep her happy. George had interviewed her several times under caution and she had been officially charged with murder. She had been incarcerated at Bronzefield to await her trial. I wondered how she was coping with conditions there after her privileged lifestyle over the last few years. I supposed she would get more than enough attention from her fellow prisoners. Perhaps she would organise singalongs like Bridget Jones.

After we emptied the van, Zak handed me a wedge of notes.

'It's all there,' he said. 'I thought you'd prefer cash. Since nothing was officially bought or sold, it might not have to go on the books.'

He winked at me, and I blushed.

'Do you still have some of that delicious coffee?' I asked to deflect Harry's attention.

'Absolutely,' said Zak. 'Kim made a loaf of banana bread too, if you're hungry.'

'I'm always hungry,' said Harry.

While Zak made the coffees, I admired his furniture for the last time. Kim followed me around as if making sure I didn't take anything. I picked up several insignificant items to examine, merely to annoy her.

'Coffee's ready,' said Zak, carrying in a tray.

I noticed Harry eying up the leather recliner, but Zak got there first. I made a mental note to be on the alert for a second-hand one. It would make a nice birthday present. Zak sighed with contentment as he sat back and munched his way through a large wedge of cake. Kim sat awkwardly on the armrest and almost got thrown off when he put the chair back. I didn't fancy her chances of a long stay.

'Are you staying in England?' I asked.

'I think so. I would like to travel around and see some of the historic sites. My grandfather came from Scotland, so I'm keen on visiting soon.'

'Wear thermals,' said Harry. 'It's chilly up north at this time of year.'

'Is there any skiing in Scotland?' said Kim. 'I want to go to Val d'Isere for the season.'

Zak's lip curled, and I revised my chances of Kim staying around long downwards. He was spoiled for choice where girls like Kim were concerned.

As soon as I finished my coffee, I checked my watch and gave a fake gasp.

'Is that the time? Harry, we must go.'

'Oh, yes, you've got that thing, haven't you?' he said, lying valiantly.

I patted my pocket to be sure I still had our cash.

'I don't suppose you want to sell me your recliner?' I said.

'Oh, please take that ratty old thing,' said Kim. 'It doesn't fit with the rest of the house at all.'

Zak sighed.

'Take it,' he said. 'I'll buy a pair of matching floral ones.'

Kim's smug smile said it all. I stood to one side with her while Harry and Zak struggled to load the chair into the back of the van.

'Are you sure about this?' asked Harry.

'Anything for some peace and quiet,' said Zak.

Harry couldn't help whistling on the way home, as I inwardly grappled with where I could fit his recliner in the sitting room of the Grotty Hovel. In the end, I removed an armchair which I put straight into Second Home to make space for Harry's 'man chair' as he insisted on calling it. The chair immediately became the focal point of Hades's search for the best seat in the house. Every time Harry wanted to sit there, he had a running battle with Hades, who refused to let him. Finally, they came to a truce, where Hades would let Harry sit as long as he could lie on top of him at any angle he felt like. Zak would have approved.

Seacastle sank back into its habitual winter gloom after the circus had departed. Roz mourned the departure of Sloane Rangers by binge watching The Traitors, and giving us a blow by blow account of the goings on whenever she could force us to listen. Ghita had her hands full with baking a production line of cakes after Zak mentioned the Vintage in an interview and we were swamped with people wanting to take selfies in the café. Some of them even bought souvenirs, so I couldn't complain. I even put some stills of the stars up on the walls along with the photographs of the musical hall stars from the Seacastle Palladium.

'He sure is handsome,' said Ghita, staring up at Zak's picture. 'I wonder if I should call him now he's single.'

'Don't you dare,' I said, channelling Cheryl Barker. 'Dangerous people, reality stars.'

~~~~~~~~~~~~~~~~~~~~

Thank you for reading my book. Please leave me a review if you enjoyed it.

Pre-order the next in the series for May 2025 – LETHAL SECRET

Other books

The Seacastle Mysteries - a cosy mystery series set on the south coast of England

Deadly Return (Book 1)
Staying away is hard, but returning may prove fatal. Tanya Bowe, a former investigative journalist, is adjusting to life as an impoverished divorcee in the seaside town of Seacastle. She crosses paths with a long-lost schoolmate, Melanie Conrad, during a house clearance to find stock for her vintage shop. The two women renew their friendship, but their reunion takes a tragic turn when Mel is found lifeless at the foot of the stairs in the same house.

While the police are quick to label Mel's death as an accident, Tanya's gut tells her there's more to the story. Driven by her instincts, she embarks on her own investigation, delving into Mel's mysterious past. As she probes deep into the Conrad family's secrets, Tanya uncovers a complex web of lies and blackmail. But the further she digs, the more intricate the puzzle becomes. As Tanya's determination grows, so does the shadow of danger. Each new revelation brings her closer to a chilling truth. Can she unravel the secrets surrounding Mel's demise before the killer strikes again?

Eternal Forest (Book 2)
What if proving a friend's husband innocent of murder implicates her instead?
Tanya Bowe, an ex-investigative journalist, and divorcee, runs a vintage shop in the coastal town of Seacastle. When her old friend, Lexi Burlington-Smythe borrows the office above the shop as a base for the campaign to create a kelp sanctuary off the coast, Tanya is thrilled with the chance to get involved and make some extra money. Tanya soon gets drawn into the high-stake arguments surrounding the campaign, as tempers are frayed, and her friends, Roz and Ghita favour opposing camps. When a celebrity eco warrior is murdered, the evidence implicates Roz's husband Ed, and Tanya finds her loyalties stretched to breaking point as she struggles to discover the true identity of the murderer.

Fatal Tribute (Book 3)
How do you find the murderer when every act is convincing?
Tanya Bowe, an ex-investigative journalist, agrees to interview the contestants of the National Talent Competition for the local newspaper, but finds herself up to her neck in secrets, sabotage and simmering resentment. The tensions increase when her condescending sister comes to stay next door for the duration of the contest.
Several rising stars on the circuit hope to win the competition, but old stager, Lance Emerald, is not going down without a fight. When Lance is found dead in his dressing room, Tanya is determined to find the murderer, but complex dynamics between the contestants and fraught family relationships make the mystery harder to solve. Can Tanya uncover the truth before another murder takes centre stage?

Toxic Vows (Book 4)
A shotgun marriage can lead to deadly celebrations
Despite her reservations, Tanya Bowe, ex-investigative journalist and local sleuth, feels obliged to plan and attend the wedding of her ex-husband DI George Carter. The atmosphere is less than convivial as underlying tensions bubble to the surface. But when the bride is found dead only hours after the ceremony, the spotlight is firmly turned onto George as the prime suspect. A reluctant Tanya is forced to come to George's aid when his rival, DI Antrim is determined to prove him responsible for her death. She discovers the bride had a lot of dangerous secrets, but so did other guests at the wedding. Did the murderer intend to kill, or have an elaborate plan gone badly wrong?

Mortal Vintage (Book 5)
Does an ancient coven hold the key to solving a murder?
Few tears are shed when the unpopular manager of the annual Seacastle Vintage Fair meets a sinister end. But local sleuth Tanya Bowe is thrust into the heart of the investigation when her friend, Grace Wong, finds herself under scrutiny for the murder. When Tanya's investigation uncovers a suspicious death in the same family, all bets are off. She navigates dark undercurrents of greed and betrayal as she uncovers a labyrinth of potential suspects associated with an ancient coven. Nothing is as it seems, and every clue adds extra complications. To solve the case, Tanya must answer one key question. Did someone hate the victim enough to kill her, or was greed the stronger motive?

Last Orders (Book 6)
Has a restaurant critic's scathing review led to his murder?
The grand opening of the Surfusion restaurant attracts a famous food critic, raising the stakes for the owners. The

night takes a dark turn when he collapses into his coffee, hours after his scathing review goes live. Local sleuth, Tanya Bowe, a friend of the owners, witnesses the shocking incident and vows to clear their names.

As Tanya digs deeper, what at first seems like an open-and-shut case against the owners unravels into a web of intrigue. Is the famous critic even the intended victim of the crime? Tanya Bowe has her work cut out for her as hidden motives lead to simmering tensions among her friends. With time running out and Surfusion's future on the line, can Tanya unmask the culprit before it's too late?

Lethal Secret (Book 8)
When old secrets resurface, danger isn't far behind...
The Shanty pub is the heart of Seacastle—a place for laughter, friendship, and the occasional small-town drama. But when a random murder occurs right outside its doors, the cozy community is shocked to the core.

Tanya Bowe thought she'd seen it all as Seacastle's local sleuth, but nothing prepares her for what comes next. Joy Wells, co-owner of the Shanty, vanishes without a trace, with only a cryptic note left behind. To the townsfolk, Joy and her husband, Ryan, are pub owners. But Tanya knows their secret—Joy and Ryan are spies, and someone from their mysterious past may be back for revenge.

With Ryan confined to a wheelchair and desperate to find his wife, Tanya and her friends follow a series of sinister clues left by Joy's captor. The hunt takes them deeper into Joy's hidden life, uncovering old betrayals and deadly secrets. As the stakes rise, Tanya must rely on her wits and courage to solve the puzzle and save her friend.

But time is running out, and every step closer to the truth raises the stakes. Will Tanya and the gang find Joy before time runs out?

Purrfect Crime – A Seacastle Christmas Novella
The purrfect Christmas mystery to keep you up all night. When preparations for Christmas at the Grotty Hovel are interrupted by the discovery of a body in the back garden, local sleuth, Tanya Bowe, finds herself embroiled in a cold case mystery. The local police are less than enthusiastic about pursuing the case before the holidays, but Tanya can't wait. Then Hades, their rescue cat, goes missing, and all festivities are put on hold as Tanya and her housemates search high and low for their pesky feline. As the hunt for Hades becomes more frantic, Tanya suspects his disappearance may be linked to the body in her garden. Who has kit-napped Hades? Will Tanya find the murderer before the turkey starts to rot?

Other books by the Author
I write under various pen names in different genres. If you are looking for another mystery, why don't you try Mortal Mission, written as Pip Skinner.

Mortal Mission
Will they find life on Mars, or death?
When the science officer for the first crewed mission to Mars dies suddenly, backup Hattie Fredericks gets the coveted place on the crew. But her presence on the Starship provokes suspicion when it coincides with a series of incidents which threaten to derail the mission.
After a near-miss while landing on the planet, the world watches as Hattie and her fellow astronauts struggle to survive. But, worse than the harsh elements on Mars, is

their growing realisation that someone, somewhere, is trying to destroy the mission.

When more astronauts die, Hattie doesn't know who to trust. And her only allies are 35 million miles away. As the tension ratchets up, violence and suspicion invade both worlds. If you like science-based sci-fi and a locked-room mystery with a twist, you'll love this book.

The Green Family Saga

Rebel Green – Book 1

Relationships fracture when two families find themselves caught up in the Irish Troubles.

The Green family move to Kilkenny from England in 1969, at the beginning of the conflict in Northern Ireland. They rent a farmhouse on the outskirts of town and make friends with the O'Connor family next door. Not every member of the family adapts easily to their new life, and their differing approaches lead to misunderstandings and friction. Despite this, the bonds between the family members deepen with time.

Perturbed by the worsening violence in the North threatening to invade their lives, the children make a pact never to let the troubles come between them. But promises can be broken, with tragic consequences for everyone.

Africa Green – Book 2

Will a white chimp save its rescuers or get them killed?

Journalist Isabella Green travels to Sierra Leone, a country emerging from civil war, to write an article about a chimp sanctuary. Animals that need saving are her obsession, and she can't resist getting involved with the project, which is on the verge of bankruptcy. She forms a bond with local boy, Ten, and army veteran, Pete, to try to save it. When they rescue a rare white chimp from a village frequented by a dangerous rebel splinter group, the resulting media interest could save the sanctuary. But the rebel group has not signed the ceasefire. They believe the voodoo power of the white chimp protects them from bullets, and they are determined to take it back so they can storm the capital. When Pete and Ten go missing, only Isabella stands in the rebels' way. Her love for the chimps unlocks the fighting spirit within her. Can she save the sanctuary or will she die trying?

Fighting Green – Book 3

Liz Green is desperate for a change. The Dot-Com boom is raging in the City of London, and she feels exhausted and out of her dcpth. Added to that, her long-term boyfriend, Sean O'Connor, is drinking too much and shows signs of going off the rails. Determined to start anew, Liz abandons both Sean and her job, and buys a near-derelict house in Ireland to renovate.

She moves to Thomastown where she renews old ties and makes new ones, including two lawyers who become rivals for her affection. When Sean's attempt to win her back goes disastrously wrong, Liz finishes with him for good. Finding herself almost penniless, and forced to seek new ways to survive, Liz is torn between making a fresh start and going back to her old loves.

Can Liz make a go of her new life, or will her past become her future?

The Sam Harris Series (written as PJ Skinner)

Set in the late 1980s and through the 1990s, the thrilling Sam Harris Adventure series navigates through the career of a female geologist. Themes such as women working in formerly male domains, and what constitutes a normal existence, are developed in the context of Sam's constant ability to find herself in the middle of an adventure or mystery. Sam's home life provides a contrast to her adventures and feeds her need to escape. Her attachment to an unfaithful boyfriend is the thread running through her romantic life, and her attempts to break free of it provide another side to her character.

The first book in the Sam Harris Series sets the scene for the career of an unwilling heroine, whose bravery and resourcefulness are needed to navigate a series of adventures set in remote sites in Africa and South America. Based loosely on the real-life adventures of the author, the settings and characters are given an authenticity that will connect with readers who enjoy adventure fiction and mysteries set in remote settings with realistic scenarios.

Fool's Gold - Book 1

Newly qualified geologist Sam Harris is a woman in a man's world - overlooked, underpaid but resilient and passionate. Desperate for her first job, and nursing a broken heart, she accepts an offer from notorious entrepreneur Mike Morton, to search for gold deposits in the remote rainforests of Sierramar. With the help of nutty local heiress Gloria Sanchez, she soon settles into life in Calderon, the capital. But when she accidentally uncovers a long-lost clue to a treasure buried deep within the jungle, her journey really begins. Teaming up with geologist Wilson Ortega, historian Alfredo Vargas and the mysterious Don Moises, they venture through the jungle, where she lurches between excitement and insecurity. Yet there is a far graver threat looming; Mike and Gloria discover that one member of the expedition is plotting to seize the fortune for himself and will do anything to get it. Can Sam survive and find the treasure, or will her first adventure be her last?

Hitler's Finger - Book 2
The second book in the Sam Harris Series sees the return of our heroine Sam Harris to Sierramar to help her friend Gloria track down her boyfriend, the historian Alfredo Vargas. Geologist Sam Harris loves getting her hands dirty. So, when she learns that her friend Alfredo has gone missing in Sierramar, she gives her personal life some much needed space and hops on the next plane. But she never expected to be following the trail of a devious Nazi plot nearly 50 years after World War II ... Deep in a remote mountain settlement, Sam must uncover the village's dark history. If she cannot reach her friend in time, the Nazi survivors will ensure Alfredo's permanent silence. Can Sam blow the lid on the conspiracy before the Third Reich makes a devastating return?

The Star of Simbako - Book 3
A fabled diamond, a jealous voodoo priestess, disturbing cultural practices. What might go wrong? The third book in the Sam Harris Series sees Sam Harris on her first contract to West Africa to Simbako, a land of tribal kingdoms and voodoo. Nursing a broken heart, Sam Harris goes to Simbako to work in the diamond fields of Fona. She is soon involved with a cast of characters who are starring in their own soap opera, a dangerous mix of superstition, cultural practices, and ignorance (mostly her own). Add a love triangle and a jealous woman who wants her dead and Sam is in trouble again. Where is the Star of Simbako? Is Sam going to survive the chaos?

The Pink Elephants - Book 4
Sam gets a call in the middle of the night that takes her to the Masaibu project in Lumbono, Africa. The project is collapsing under the weight of corruption and chicanery engendered by management, both in country

and back on the main company board. Sam has to navigate murky waters to get it back on course, not helped by interference from people who want her to fail. When poachers invade the elephant sanctuary next door, her problems multiply. Can Sam protect the elephants and save the project or will she have to choose?

The Bonita Protocol - Book 5

An erratic boss. Suspicious results. Stock market shenanigans. Can Sam Harris expose the scam before they silence her? It's 1996. Geologist Sam Harris has been around the block, but she's prone to nostalgia, so she snatches the chance to work in Sierramar, her old stomping ground. But she never expected to be working for a company that is breaking all the rules. When the analysis results from drill samples are suspiciously high, Sam makes a decision that puts her life in peril. Can she blow the lid on the conspiracy before they shut her up for good?

Digging Deeper - Book 6

A feisty geologist working in the diamond fields of West Africa is kidnapped by rebels. Can she survive the ordeal, or will this adventure be her last? It's 1998. Geologist Sam Harris is desperate for money, so she takes a job in a tinpot mining company working in war-torn Tamazia. But she never expected to be kidnapped by blood thirsty rebels.

Working in Gemsite would never be easy with its culture of misogyny and corruption. Her boss, the notorious Adrian Black is engaged in a game of cat and mouse with the government over taxation. Just when Sam makes a breakthrough, the camp is overrun by rebels and Sam is taken captive. Will anyone bother to rescue her, and will she still be alive if they do?

Concrete Jungle - Book 7 (series end)
Armed with an MBA, Sam Harris is storming the City - But has she swapped one jungle for another?
Forging a new career would never be easy, and Sam discovers she has not escaped from the culture of misogyny and corruption that blighted her field career.
When her past is revealed, she finally achieves the acceptance she has always craved, but being one of the boys is not the panacea she expected. The death of a new friend presents her with the stark choice of compromising her principals to keep her new position, or exposing the truth behind the façade. Will she finally get what she wants or was it all a mirage?
Box Sets

Sam Harris Adventure Box Set Book 2-4
Sam Harris Adventure Box Set Book 5-7
Sam Harris Adventure Box Set Books 2-7

Connect with the Author

Before I wrote novels, I spent 30 years working as an exploration geologist, managing projects on the ground, and doing due diligence in over thirty countries. During this time, I collected the tall tales and real-life experiences which inspired the Sam Harris Adventure Series, chronicling the adventures of a female geologist as a pioneer in a hitherto exclusively male world.

Then, my childhood in Ireland inspired me to write the Green Family Saga (as Kate Foley), which follows the fortunes of an English family who move to Ireland before the start of the troubles.

I moved to the south coast of England before the Covid pandemic. After finishing my Irish trilogy, I was inspired to write a mystery on Mars, Mortal Mission, inspired by the landing of the Mars Rover. It is a science-based murder mystery, think "The Martian" with fewer potatoes and more bodies.

Having thoroughly enjoyed writing my first mystery, I decided to write a whole series. As I am not a fan of graphic violence or sex, it was inevitable I should be a Cosy Mystery writer. I have always been a massive fan of crime and mystery and I guess it was inevitable I would turn my hand to this genre eventually. And so the Seacastle Mysteries were born.

Follow me on Amazon to get informed of my new releases. Put PJ Skinner into the search box on Amazon and then click on the follow button on my author page.

Please subscribe to my Seacastle Mysteries Newsletter for updates and offers by using this QR code

You can also use the QR code below to get to my website for updates and to buy paperbacks direct from me.

You can also follow me on Twitter, Instagram or on Facebook @pjskinnerauthor